The
Veiled
Sultan

*By the same Author*

I, RACHEL
JUBILEE OF A GHOST
AFTER THE FESTIVAL
THE YEAR OF THE YIELD
THE COUNTESS
THE BESPOKEN MILE
THE DARK STAR
PERIOD PIECES
THE BITTER GREEN OF THE WILLOW
THE INTERPRETER
A WOMAN OF LETTERS
HER GRACE PRESENTS
THE UNKNOWN ANGEL
INVITATION FROM MINERVA
THE HOUR AWAITS
THE DARK GLASS
A MAN NAMED LUKE

# The Veiled Sultan

MARCH COST 

*Author of "I, Rachel," etc.*



New York
THE VANGUARD PRESS, INC.

Standard Book Number 8149-0666-4
Library of Congress Catalog Card Number 76-99494


Manufactured in the United States of America.

To
DESMOND FLOWER
with remembrance

'Political genius was sometimes greatly developed with the favourite Sultanas, who were admitted to all the confidences of government, and took part in all the intrigues of Court. Long and great reigns have been founded and governed by some one of these beautiful slaves, perpetuating in the palace the ascendency of their charms by the ascendency of their genius. Favourites, they enslaved; mothers they planned in secret and prepared for the reigns of their sons.'

Lamartine

'It is precisely because the Orient covers them with a veil and silence, that women are of greatest effectiveness in the most delicate negotiations, a subtle influence radiating only in the shadow.'

Cadalvene and Barrault

# CONTENTS

# FOREWORD

MANY years ago during my researches on Count Rumford's life I came across a reference to the amazing life-story of Aimée Dubuc de Rivery, the French convent pupil kidnapped on the high seas for the Sultan's Harem—one of the most remarkable women in history and the woman who, eventually, became the mother of the Sultan Mahmoud, imperial reformer.

After reading a comprehensive account of her life and that of her son in a delightful book by Benjamin A. Morton, entitled *The Veiled Empress*, published by Putnam in 1923, I spent nearly a year's research on the subject before writing a play on which an option was taken by a well-known American opera company. I followed the known historical facts closely, except in the instance of the Sultan Abdul Hamid's age when the play opened, and for the fact that in the play he met the fate of his nephew Selim—as neither of these changes affected Aimée's rise to imperial power as the mother of Mahmoud. Although the option on my play was not exercised, the story continued to fascinate me, and on the suggestion of my American agent I decided to write it as a novel. By this time I had also read with the liveliest interest Lesley Blanch's historical survey of Aimée's life in *The Wilder Shores of Love,* but my present book is not another outline of the startling facts already ably recorded by others and also attested by Sir Walter Scott, who had heard of the Martinique fortune-teller's prediction of a throne for Aimée's cousin Joséphine too, long before both predictions came to pass. This book is my interpretation of how these amazing events of comedy and tragedy must have affected those most closely involved—the drama itself, in fact.

For this purpose I have taken the leaves of a lost memoir—as what is more likely than that Aimée kept a diary in the loneliness of her life as a foreigner in the Harem? This memoir comes to an end five years before her death for, as the Veiled Sultan, beset with the State exactions of her imperial position, she can have had little leisure latterly for anything but her prayers. Although denied a priest throughout her lifetime in the Harem, these prayers we know she never neglected. Mr Morton vividly relates in his book that late on a certain wild winter's night in 1817, Father Chrysostome, Superior of the Monastery of St Antoine, was startled by a secret summons, an imperial firman, presented by two Palace Guards, to cross the Golden

Horn at once in an imperial caique. Buffeted by a fierce storm, and to his increasing dismay and amazement, he was finally conducted through the darkness to an unknown destination of the greatest luxury. In a chamber of sombre magnificence he found a dying woman lying on a sumptuous bed, with a Greek doctor in attendance. Nearby stood a tall man who might have been forty years of age (he was in reality thirty-two)—his brow noble, his expression austere, his attire simple but of striking elegance. Signing to the doctor and the slaves to withdraw, this man then advanced to the bed and, in a voice shaken by emotion, said: 'My Mother, you have wished to die in the religion of your fathers. Let your wish be fulfilled.' For an hour the priest remained there, praying with the woman. Then, as her life ebbed, he administered the last rites. At the final words the silent witness of this astounding scene stepped forward once again and fell on his knees, his brow to the ground, calling upon Allah in his grief. . .

Later, Father Chrysostome was conveyed back to his monastery with the same secrecy as before, having to his own stupefaction sped the soul of the Veiled Sultan according to the rites of the Church of Rome from the hitherto unbroken fastness of the Seraglio.

She is buried, as Mr Morton records in his book, within the sacred enclosure of the Mosque of

Mohammed II, on the summit of the fourth hill of Constantinople, and in one of the most magnificent of the imperial Turbehs. Its lengthy epitaph in verse, dedicated to Naksh, the Beautiful, was probably composed by Mahmoud, her son, who was himself a poet.

But her treasured breviary, her hidden rosary—where did those precious tokens vanish, as Sultan succeeded Sultan? As Father Chrysostome's experience reappeared years later in a provincial French newspaper of the early nineteenth century, I have sometimes thought that the precious breviary and rosary may yet reappear also—perhaps in the dusty glass case of some Turkish museum, with the lost leaves of the memoir—which, written in the French language, must long ago have seemed to officialdom simply some forgotten romance.

# 1. THE CONVENT

GROWING older, the past sometimes grows clearer, like a belated dawn, a revisitation of youth, and while this freshness is upon me I write these recollections.

As every Prince of Turkey must adopt a profession, and you, my son, have chosen that of scribe, you may later feel a tender sympathy for this memoir, even for its calligraphy so unlike the perfection of your own now ornamenting our state memorials.

There is, too, the hope that your children will one day read it and draw nearer us in understanding bygone difficulties. . .

Here then are some remembrances of a child, of a girl closer to you than anyone, and whom yet you never knew as such—in what must surely be one of the strangest destinies that ever befell a woman.

I was an orphan, twelve years old, when I sailed in 1776 from Martinique with my guardian, M. Dubuc de Sainte Preuve, and my maid Blanche, the Negress—on my way to the Convent at Nantes, to complete my education. The eight years that followed at the Convent of the Dames de la Visitation are still more vivid than the twelve years that preceded these in the tropical languor of Martinique. There, my cousin and companion, Marie-Joseph, who later became Joséphine, Empress of the French, alone stands out dynamically in those earlier dreamy days among the rich French families of the colony.

I can remember that last day at the Convent at Nantes in 1784, when I was almost twenty-one, as if it were yesterday! My room faced the garden, not the cloister, as I was simply a student at this exclusive house. Sometimes the muted rumble of the city across its cobbles reached me, but on that last spring morning in France the moist wind was in the other direction and only church bells could be heard, and a blackbird fluting. . . .

I still wore the black convent garb and short head-veil of ladies in retreat when I ran from the garden, my hands full of flowers, to brighten the prim Convent parlour. Two windows framed the garden, and between them stood the open garden door. On the left wall, so that you can see it clearly, my son, there was a latticed window-grille, shuttered just then. Opposite was the door which led to my bedroom. But apart from a table and some upright chairs, a small bookcase and a prie-dieu, it was a bare, almost drab room. Yet I had been very happy there. Constantly, to the amusement of the sisters, I would devise ways of brightening it. Hastily now I began to arrange the violets and primroses in a little bowl for them—

Just then the wooden shutter behind the wall-grille slid back noisily, and a quiet voice said:

'Reverend Mother will be with you at once.'

Guiltily I tried to adjust my head-veil and to tidy the table of its strewn flowers, but as always that tall unhurried figure was too fleet for me!

'Good morning, my child . . . still painting the lily!'

She was a calm, smiling woman with a touch of mockery in her manner. A certain crispness in speech suggested that impatience might once have been a temptation, but precision was now its only indication. Looking back, I realize that she had re-created herself with a very firm hand and remained vigilance itself. Then I simply curtseyed quickly, 'Ah, Reverend Mother, if only I'd finished the bowl, it would have looked perfect and then been almost invisible!'

Together we laughed and then I saw that she was carrying a handsome leather portfolio which she laid on the table. 'None the less,' she said, 'we shall miss your flowery ways.'

'As I shall miss this blessed home, Reverend Mother—more than words can say.'

Dryly she retorted, 'You will recover—possibly before we do. Eight years is eight years for us. Here are your papers for the journey and all your scholastic reports. Your guardian at Martinique will see how highly we esteem you. I have also commended your patience during these past twelve months. You might have sailed after the peace treaty was signed, but you accepted my advice with a good grace.'

Between a gasp and a laugh I confessed: 'No, no, I was thankful to run no risk then! I might have been captured by the British at sea—worse still, by the Barbary Corsairs.'

Crisply she said: 'Fear is faith in misfortune—it should be dismissed. But frankness shows courage, and in bidding goodbye I find much to commend. In fact,' again her tone was ironical, 'during this past year you might have passed for the perfect postulant.'

Confused, I stammered, 'Oh, Reverend Mother, that was a dream, a hope, an aspiration of mine that passed too soon. But *you* knew all along that I had no true vocation—that I was not worthy.'

'Eighteen is a susceptible age,' she said sharply, 'that is all I told you then.'

'Yes,' I whispered, 'and so it proved. I'm now ashamed of my presumption, for in a few months the urge for—for freedom asserted itself. I knew that when the time came, I must leave.'

'The urge for freedom is another illusion—as you will realize when you have tried your wings. But to be bound, and yet free, is the very door of bliss.'

I gazed at her in awe. 'Bound and yet free . . . that

must be the secret of life. Listening to you now—I almost feel I should not sail!'

Unmoved, she continued: 'But between those two states, bound and yet free, there is often a long journey. Now, before you leave, a final word on two issues. First you must check, once and for all, your tendency to tears.'

'Yes,' I hung my head, 'I know it is a weakness.'

'It is less a weakness than a weapon,' she said shortly. 'Perhaps the paltriest of our sex. Avoid it as you would Satan himself—for it will end by enslaving no one but yourself. In the whole course of my charge—and some of the sisters have been tearful terrors—I have never known anyone who wept with your fluency!'

Fervently I replied, 'Reverend Mother, from this minute I'll do my utmost to remember that I am a Dubuc de Rivery, and that my ancestors fought in the Crusades.'

'To remember that you are not an ornamental cistern should suffice. Secondly, the climate of Martinique is enervating, so check any tendency to overeat.'

I was aghast. 'Reverend Mother! What a dreadful thought—oh, surely I have never been guilty of gluttony here?'

Pleasantly she said, 'The fifth of the seven deadly sins. I see I have shocked you. You will not forget so readily. Apart from those two dangers—devoutly accept life as it comes. Remember the words of St Gregory of Sinai—and do not reject what is at hand to dream of something else.'

More soberly I said, 'Yes, Reverend Mother, I think I shall remember.'

At that she gave me a steady look which I have never forgotten. 'I think you will. Meantime Madame de Beauharnais has arrived to say goodbye, and your maid is anxious to dress you. But I think it wiser that Madame de Beauharnais sees you first in our convent garb. It is some time since you met and your cousin is still embroiled in worldly difficulties.'

Eagerly I assured her, 'But I am certain that she is not to blame for her misfortunes since marriage. I know her better than anyone. She has been more to me than any sister. Believe me, Joséphine is pure gold.'

'No need to paint *that* lily then! And I make no secret of my relief that at *present* she will only accompany you to the jetty. So now—goodbye!'

'Reverend Mother, after eight years—' I found myself faltering, 'thank you from the heart for all you have done for me. I shall often feel lost without you—' and I dropped to my knees. 'Bless me before I go.'

Quietly she made the sign of the Cross upon me. 'Go in peace, my child, and remain in peace. You have the virtue of constancy—there you will not be tempted so often.' Gently she raised me to my feet and, with a brief nod of approval, left me.

Bereft, I stood gazing after her—when suddenly the shutter behind the grille flew back and the extern-sister announced:

'Madame de Beauharnais is here. You have ten minutes together before you dress for your journey.'

The door to the right of the grille opened, and my cousin ran to meet me. We were the same age, but Joséphine looked older because of her elegance and sophistication. Quietly but modishly dressed, her grace and beauty had a restless energy that compelled attention. Although her skin was clear and her hair of a rich chestnut colour, she always insisted that she looked dark beside my startling fairness. I realize now that there was another difference, for she was essentially worldly-wise but reckless, while I was both childishly romantic yet practical. But Joséphine, despite her vagaries, invariably retained a curious personal dignity that was possibly part of our family heritage.

With a cry of gladness we ran into each other's arms.

'My darling Aimée, I should have been here last night, but first the Paris coach was delayed and then the diligence. Everything seemed against our meeting! Even here—at the Convent—they have kept me waiting.'

'That you should have made such a journey to

see me off'—again we embraced, and then sat down laughing at the table like a couple of schoolgirls.

'If *only* I were coming all the way—but in a year or so when my baby is older I shall return to Martinique. I have sworn it! Oh, Aimée, Hortense is such a pretty child—little Eugène's nose is already out of joint!'

'Never! I shall love him twice as much to make up —after all, he came first.'

'Before I forget—here is a box of bon-bons for the journey.'

'From the size, I thought it was a hat box! Bon-bons, how delicious! Oh, dear me, I must remember—'

'Remember what?'

'That I tend to pamper myself. But I shall share them with the other passengers . . . perhaps the crew as well.'

'My poor dear, it's high time you were out of here and had some real peccadilloes to repent!'

I burst out laughing. 'What a fate—to be either a little pig or a little prig! Give me your news.'

'It's as good as any misfortune can be. At last I have won my case against my husband. The Provost has ordered him not only to respect our separation but to pay for the support of the two children. The Provost's decrees vindicate me before the whole world. No one will ever know all I've been through—'

and she gave a shudder. 'Had it not been for the kindness of *his* family, I could not have survived. Take it from me, Aimée, that when one's in-laws side with you, things are as bad as they can be! At first they blamed that fiend of a woman, his mistress, but later they had to admit that he too was beyond forgiveness. After he dared to state publicly that Hortense was not his child!'

'*Joséphine!*'

'Oh, you haven't heard half of it yet. But now the Provost's findings have clinched his responsibility.'

'And to think how you loved him once—that gallant young captain in his white uniform!'

Joséphine turned away her head. 'There was something I never told you. A horrible shock at the very start. That hateful woman was there the whole time. Even on the honeymoon he saw her. At first I made scenes. A jealous woman will suspect her own shadow, he said. *Shadow*! She was a daily reality. I have endured hell.'

'Merciful heaven, and you so dear, so good, so beautiful—the man must be a monster—'

'No, he's merely a man, and men are very different from our early dreams, Aimée. What I could tell you! But this is scarcely the place to open my heart—'

'You were married too young,' I began.

'I was full of hope—and glad to escape.'

'To escape?' I was astonished.

'Yes. Father indulged me, but Mother detested me. Existence at home was a prolonged squabble. I used to dream of another kind of life—and freedom.'

Slowly I said, 'They say to dream is dangerous.'

She shrugged. 'It certainly landed *me* out of the frying pan into the fire! You are an orphan, Aimée, but Monsieur Dubuc de Sainte Preuve has been a wise and kindly guardian. Serenity is more important for children than love or indulgence, so I shall rejoin you at Martinique with my two darlings, where we can exist more cheaply, too—'

'I'll live for that,' I told her earnestly. 'From the first days you were there. I feel you will be with me to the last. I think of you always as my sister-self. But what you must have suffered!'

Flippantly she said, 'I admit one recovers more quickly when one's heart is broken privately. Publicity is an added ordeal—' she suddenly buried her face in her hands. Then, as quickly again, she sat up coldly. 'Happily my heart is now as hollow as a drum. It can only give off echoes—war-like ones, I'm afraid!'

Indignantly I assured her: 'You are listening to *his* empty heart—not your own. If you must listen to another heart, listen to mine. See!' and I opened a small gold locket which I wore around my neck. 'A heart that opens to reveal two hearts—in one is your portrait, in the other your little son. My heart supports them both. It will beat for you and yours forever!'

Surprised and touched, she examined the locket. 'You always had an ardent nature. Strange, if in the end you were to prove more faithful than any man. Strange—and a little disappointing!' Together we burst out laughing again.

'My first laugh in a hundred years! Oh, Aimée, what merry times we always had together. If you only knew how I long to laugh. Do you remember our visit to that fortune-teller, Euphémie David, before you left Martinique?'

Fondly I nodded: 'The little hut was smothered in tropical growth, and we were terrified of the old Negress because her predictions were known to come true. But we braved it out—and entered.'

Joséphine was still laughing. 'We were each promised a throne, remember? Nothing less than that! And here am I, already separated from my husband, my life in ruins—and you, through the delay of war, *returning* to Martinique and nothing more exciting than a basket-chair on the balcony.'

Just for a second, I hesitated. 'There's something you've forgotten. She promised you two husbands. A fair man and a dark man. A lawsuit would separate you from the first, she said, who would later perish in a tragic fashion.'

Joséphine was suddenly alert. 'How on earth could I have forgotten that? It was from the second husband that the throne would come. And she certainly said that by my first husband I should have two children. Ah! now I know why I've forgotten those details! After astonishing the world with the dark gentleman—those were her very words—she said I should die unhappy. No wonder I forgot. She gave me a tragic run for my money. I don't think your fate was much better?'

Slowly I said: 'I was to occupy a vast and magnificent palace—in supreme dignity. I was to have a son who would reign gloriously, but at the height of my happiness my life on earth would vanish like a dream. There was more to it, but for the moment it escapes me.'

'No wonder! A lot of twaddle. Yet everyone on the island lapped it up. My dear, believe it or not, when my ship sailed from Martinique and that meteor she had prophesied appeared above it, with phosphorescent light around our masts, even the crew believed it was a sign from heaven. Heaven! ludicrous—'

At that moment the wooden shutter again flew back behind the grille, and at the noise Joséphine started violently. The extern-sister said quietly:

'Madame de Beauharnais, it is time to go. Mademoiselle de Rivery must dress for the voyage,' and the shutter closed.

Anxiously I asked: 'Will you wait here or in the garden?'

'In the garden. That jack-in-the-box behind us would get me down! My poor dear, you certainly live by rule here—' As Joséphine reached the garden door she called back: 'Be as quick as you can. I've more to tell you and there's little time left—'

Just then Blanche, my maid, bustled in by the door to the left of the grille with my new gown over her arm and, in the other hand, my frilled bonnet with blue velvet ribbon. She was a big, burly Negress of much dignity who had come from Martinique with me. Over her gay print dress with its wide sweeping skirt she wore a silk neckerchief, as she too was travelling that day, and a vivid little turban, the tête madras of Martinique. She was always a riot of colour in the sedate Convent parlour —a tulip in a herb-garden.

'Mamzelle Honey, we are as good as gone! And will I be glad to board that boat although I am the world's worst sailor! Now, what do you think—the Lady Prioress has written me a "character" for Monsieur Dubuc who has known me since I was a baby! These poor ladies have no notion of the meaning of language. She has written: *Blanche is an honest, energetic woman, not without humour, and at a pinch might show courage!* At a pinch!' and Blanche rolled her eyes in horror. 'What's more, Mamzelle, it's too short for my character. There's more to me than that!'

'I should say so—yards and yards more,' and I

picked up the hem of her skirt and skipped with her into the bedroom, as Blanche for a heavy woman was surprisingly buoyant on her feet.

While I dressed, I heard the church clock strike eleven, and from the cloister the patter of the novices' feet as they took up their position in the garden to bid me farewell, each in her white serge habit and white veil, with a surprise gift that had already cost weeks of planning and in which I had already pleasurably participated. One, I knew, brought a parasol, one a pair of gloves, one a lace handkerchief, one a posy—and my oldest friend there bore a guitar, for I was musical. And finally in the procession there would be the Mistress of Novices with the Convent's gift of a breviary.

Acting on impulse, for now I had a sudden longing to be the last to leave the little parlour, I told Blanche to precede me. Out she strode into the garden, with my hat box and her own striped umbrella, to the chirrups and cheers of the novices there.

I stood alone in the silence, for once like a young lady of fashion, and carrying only the handsome portfolio—at first full of the consequence of travel. Then the deserted room caught me in its memories, the table, the bookcase, the prie-dieu—

Suddenly the wooden shutter opened abruptly and revealed the Mother Superior behind the grille. I could scarcely believe my eyes at this honour and ran forward weeping—

'Reverend Mother, I can hardly bear to go.'

'No tears,' she said sharply, 'we were resolved.'

But unexpectedly I stood my ground. 'There *is* a time for tears, and this has come. I am not ashamed of these—nor need *you* be.' And somewhat to my own surprise, my voice was firm.

She smiled. 'Your discipline flatters me more. You have learned a valuable lesson here.'

Sadly I shook my head: 'I cannot feel that I have learned it.'

Dryly she said, 'You have made an admirable start, and doubtless there will be other opportunities!'

'Not too many I hope!' and I dabbed my eyes.

Briskly she said, 'In a climate like Martinique's, you cannot hope for too much exercise—or you will fall asleep on your feet!'

Just then the postillion's horn sounded and I heard my cousin's excited voice calling: 'The coach!'

I turned. Joséphine had run to the garden door and was waving me to come. 'The coach!' she called again—and then saw the Mother Superior at the grille. For a second they exchanged a look which I shall always remember. 'The coach,' Joséphine repeated, and then paused, irresolute.

'Reverend Mother,' I whispered. 'I have been so safe, so happy here. This long journey . . . I fear—I wish that it were over!'

Mildly now she said, 'All life is a journey, my

child. Goodbye. This is the day which the Lord has made. We will rejoice in it and be glad.'

'Yes, Reverend Mother,' with an effort I repeated mechanically, 'we will rejoice in it and be glad.' Curtseying deeply, I moved backwards to the garden door. She remained at the open grille to the last. I had completely forgotten Joséphine—in any case she was no longer at the garden door. But from the garden gate came the postillion's horn with an insistence that haunts me still. . .

## 2. THE HIGH SEAS

As well it might! That horn was a summons to a series of misfortunes—and the first calamity was such a storm in the Bay of Biscay that our ship finally foundered. Absurd as it now seems—Blanche and I scarcely cared, so prostrate were we with sea-sickness. Nor had we any gratitude for a miracle when, overhauled by a Spanish trader, we were, with other passengers, swung aboard the rescue ship.

But the storm abated, and this proved a superior vessel. Next day we had recovered and, basking in sunshine on deck, accepted the fact that we were now off course and must start our journey afresh from Majorca.

Then, when within sight of land, we saw across a clear sea, to the horror of all aboard, Corsair galleys swooping to head us off. My nightmare had come true. Fear, our Mother Superior had said, was faith in misfortune. . .

Yet, as the Corsairs boarded us, so unexpectedly jovial was their attitude to the passengers that we still hoped for the best.

The best! The best was the fortress of the Dey of Algiers. This was the dire misfortune which led me inescapably to much misery, then years of happiness, one agonizing sorrow, and finally to the bliss of revelation.

To all of this the postillion's horn summoned me on that moist spring morning at Nantes.

## 3. THE FORTRESS

ONE week later, still imprisoned in our own ship as it lay at anchor at Algiers, we were led across the gangway and uphill to the fortress, the stronghold of the Dey, Baba Mohammed—who for years had been the menace of the Mediterranean. Yet even then, so politely had the passengers been treated, we could not credit that the worst would now befall us.

As I mounted the last steep stone stairway in the blazing sun, I only knew that the grim façade of the fortress cast a welcome shadow.

This wall had a formidable row of pillars, and at the top of the stairs, beneath this arcade, sat a Corsair officer at a table, shouting his instructions at intervals. These commands were repeated by another voice at the far end of the arcade—apparently down another flight of stairs, for we could hear the muffled echo of yet a third voice vociferating each order. Then, and only then, did I sicken with a fear that I can still remember—clammier, I am certain, than the chill of any grave.

Barely had I reached the top of the steps with Blanche than I saw less favoured prisoners from our ship, who had mounted by another stairway behind the seated officer, being rushed along the arcade. French and Spanish naval officers and other ratings in chains, together with humbler passengers —among these a mother with two terrified children.

Automatically the seated officer called out: 'To the Hulks', in the case of the seamen, 'State Prison', in the case of the officers, 'Bazaar' or 'Market' in the case of the women. Although some of the prisoners struggled, they were silently overpowered by their guards, and the ugly scene went with the expedition of cattle relentlessly driven into different pens downstairs. Nothing prevailed except the order monotonously repeated: 'State Prison', 'State Prison', 'To the Hulks', 'Market', 'Hulks . . .'

Then, turning, the officer caught sight of my ashen face. He rose, went to a door below the arcade, opened it, and called: 'Sir, the passenger from the Convent at Nantes, with servant.'

He had spoken in French, and suddenly I regained command of myself. 'Blanche,' I said, 'have no fear. I have none. Only anger. We will prevail.'

Hurriedly she whispered: 'You're beyond belief, Mamzelle. Pray you don't sober too soon! You're surely scaring me—'

'Sir,' the Corsair officer called again, 'the passenger from the Convent at Nantes!'

The next moment his Captain, carrying my portfolio, appeared through the pillars with an elderly dignitary whose features were as fierce as his manner was frigid. Instantly I knew this must be the Dey, Baba Mohammed, and the terrifying nature of my whole encounter with this notorious man was that although he was near enough to touch me, not once did he reply to me or give any evidence of hearing me. I might already have been an object set up in the market-place.

'This is the lady,' announced the Captain, 'out of the usual run you see—an aristocrat, as her credentials confirm. Norman-French, but it seems her family, now in Martinique, are only moderately rich.'

'So much the better,' said the Dey. 'How did she come to be on the Spanish ship?'

'Her own, a small vessel bound for Martinique, sprang a leak in the Bay of Biscay. The Spanish ship went to their rescue. Later we overhauled and attacked—' he added with satisfaction, 'not a man lost.'

'Sir,' I exclaimed, 'we are French and Spanish subjects travelling on our lawful occasions. I demand our right to see the French Consul.'

Neither man made any reply. The Dey walked coldly round me, pushing Blanche aside like a bale—so that she was now separated from me. Then, frowning, he picked up one of my golden curls, rubbing it between his fingers before dropping it as perfunctorily.

'You have not exaggerated,' he told the Captain. 'She will answer my purpose well enough.'

'If I may say so, sir,' the Captain said, 'we have here a most unusual slave—beautiful, highly educated, and fresh from the Convent at Nantes. Candidly, worth a ransom.'

At this I lost total command—but for once not in tears. I heard myself shriek: 'Slave! I'll die first—barbarians!'

Blanche ran forward, whispering, 'Mamzelle, don't upset this gentleman. No harm in a little smile.'

Instantly the Captain pushed Blanche back. The Dey, unmoved, told him: 'See that her portfolio is not lost.'

'Monsters!' and now I was beyond myself, 'you will pay for this yet!'

The Captain, amused, merely remarked: 'A spirited filly, as you see, sir.'

'She'll do,' the Dey replied. 'A change from his sugary odalisques. Those last munitions from Turkey were timely. I intend her for the Sultan himself. Send her on a ship of state. Dress her in oriental clothes. Afford her every courtesy.'

'For the Grand Signior?' the Captain exclaimed. 'A graceful compliment. At once, sir.'

'Barbarian!' I cried again. 'My country will avenge us.'

But I might have been a deaf mute for any attention that they paid. 'She may prove useful to him in another way,' the Dey continued, 'as a French dictionary. But see that the book is richly bound. Spare no expense. Convey her as quickly as possible to the Sublime Porte.'

'And the servant, sir?'

There was a moment's hideous suspense, in which Blanche pitifully bobbed a curtsey to the Dey. She alone had kept her head.

For the first time the Dey laughed. 'Send the maid with her. Fewer ripples with one stone!' and he walked off, down the stairs up which I had come.

As I stood there, stiff with shock, the Captain called to the officer at the table:

'To the Sultan—afford her every courtesy.'

At once the officer at the table shouted to those at the far end of the arcade. 'For the Sublime Porte! Afford her every courtesy. To the Sultan.'

The Captain, with a bow, offered me his arm to the top of the unknown stairs. Barely touching his sleeve with my fingers, and with Blanche behind me, I moved forward like an automaton—in a stony silence now and as if I were treading through heavy water.

As I did so, I could hear the repetitions of the command echoing from below, as a drowning knell: 'For the Sublime Porte . . .' 'To the Sultan . . . To the Sultan!'

## 4. THE VOYAGE

THAT long luxurious voyage, so different from the previous one, passed like some uneasy sleep, between dream and nightmare. I had become a pendulum alternating between hope and despair—

There might yet be some miraculous rescue at sea . . . or there might not! And indeed we had not been two days out before it seemed to me that other shipping gave us as wide a berth as possible.

Earlier Blanche had been warned, before we actually set foot on the gangway, that if I as much as attempted escape or suicide her life would at once be forfeit. I do not think that this threat alarmed her—we knew each other to be realists.

Tunis, Sicily, Greece, and Aegean isles—at any port I was closely confined with her in my cabin. But no sooner were we at sea again than I was free to enjoy the pleasant awning and silken couch arranged for me on deck.

With a light following wind and brilliant sunshine the voyage might have been idyllic, as my every comfort was solicitously anticipated. But the unaccustomed oriental garments were a constant reminder of the fate awaiting me—and if for an hour my misery lessened, Blanche's ludicrous optimism never failed to work me into a frenzy again. The Sultan, she persisted, might yet prove more agreeable than I feared. No man was to be known but by experience—not even a Frenchman. All marriage was a lottery—

'*Marriage*!' I could not contain my indignation, 'a potentate with possibly a hundred wives, and you talk of marriage!'

'But, Mamzelle, with so many ladies, you're certain to see less of him. Who knows—perhaps now he is a very old gentleman who only wishes to take tea with you.'

Darkly I said, 'It's true I've no idea how old he is. All my Turkish history stopped short at the Crusades. It's lamentable—the Convent should have gone further. But if I fail to bribe someone on the harbour to take my letter to the Consul—my one and only hope will be the Sultan's advanced age. Then possibly he may take pity . . . I might persuade him to release me.'

'You keep hoping, Mamzelle. You're going to turn him round your little finger yet!'

Again I was outraged by this flagrant cheer. '*Blanche*, the man is a barbarian, an infidel—it is I, remember, who am to be sacrificed—not you! It is for me to say whether this calamity has a brighter side or not—' and I would burst into a torrent of tears from which I later slept, exhausted.

Yet such is the resilience of youth that when the hour of arrival came I was spell-bound by my first glimpse of Constantinople—its glittering domes and minarets rising like a visible paean of praise above the dense shipping of the Porte. Then, turning, I saw the hilly wooded terraces of that fabled promontory washed by the waters of the Bosphorus and Golden Horn—

There, in regal isolation, land-locked in matchless beauty, soared a region of palaces and pleasure-gardens—up, up, up to a quivering blue sky that held the hyacinth of heaven.

Awestruck despite myself, and hypnotized also by the fact that throughout the voyage I had been afforded by both Captain and crew the deference due to royalty, I next witnessed this courtesy on all sides grow warm with congratulation! In fact, such a sense of festivity now enlivened the atmosphere of the ship's approach that for an hour I completely forgot my letter to the Consul so carefully secreted on my person. And much good would it have done me anyway! No onlooker at the Porte was ever to witness my arrival for, heavily veiled, I was gently lowered, with Blanche, into a gilded caique, manned by twelve oarsmen, which swept us at the command of their Turkish naval officer to a private jetty on that distant promontory. The last object to be ceremoniously handed over by the Captain to this Turkish officer was my handsome portfolio, the gift of the Convent, and which had not once been in my possession since I was taken prisoner.

From the jetty I was finally borne upwards in a sedan chair, with Blanche behind me in another—through densely wooded terraces.

Incredible as it may seem, such was the beauty of the scene, the smiling calm of the officials who greeted me at each point of this lengthy ascent, the efficiency, above all the gentle courtesy on every hand, that I found myself temporarily lulled. Whatever else it might be, this arrival was very different from the horror of the fortress at Algiers.

In the level radiance of a golden sunset we ultimately reached a certain garden summit, and again I had an inexplicable sense of reassurance. For one thing, the quiet of those green parterres, the sunlit calm of the pillared entrance, the absence of any onlookers, except our Turkish officer and the bearers, gave a comforting impression that I was arriving at my own private residence—

True, some other white-clad officers awaited us in the atrium, with a few silent slaves, but here the same smiling calm prevailed as in the garden, still sunlit through the archways, still murmurous with doves settling to sleep. . .

It was utterly unlike anything I had imagined,

and although springtime by the calendar, here it had been a day of early summer heat.

In a dream-like daze I walked, hot and exhausted, into a suite of rooms where elegance and a cool simplicity were one. I was beyond noting other details then, but I still remember that the only sound there was the tinkle of an indoor fountain.

With Blanche's help I undressed, bathed, and then, stunned by sleep, fell across my bed.

For the first and only time in my life I slept the round of the clock.

# 5. THE ARRIVAL

Two days later I was to find myself in a much less thankful state of mind. My reassurance had vanished as mysteriously as it had come. I was again alone with my situation—to the outward eye, admittedly, that of an earthly paradise. Yet, without once entering the garden or leaving that suite of rooms, already I knew that this was not the separate residence I had hoped—but the wing of a much larger building from which, by noiseless slaves in spotless attire, delectable meals were brought us at regular intervals.

Our bedrooms faced sheerly over wooded terraces to the sea, but the view from the reception chamber disclosed, through a small arched window to the right, azure sky above the garden, while a much larger window, also unglazed, overlooked a wide paved court with an avenue beyond. These windows were set high, and even tall Blanche had to stand on a hassock to see out, while I had to mount upon the divan to look at the court and avenue, both of which remained completely silent. Shortly this quietude increased my uneasiness. Then too I had discovered that a sentry was posted night and day outside the entrance to my suite, facing the atrium, where the fountain tinkled. The garden and bedroom aspects were without any visible sentry, as no doubt the steep face of those terraces below formed its own fortress.

The charm of this spacious white-walled reception chamber was lost on me—for all was alien: the olive-green divan piled with brocaded cushions, the low jade table intricately carved, the alabaster lamp on its gold tripod—and not another object but an ornate prayer carpet, its apex facing east on the tiled floor. Doors did not exist. The only entrance to the atrium beyond was a latticed Moorish gate, at present concealed from sight by a crimson velvet curtain.

My anxiety had mounted on this third day as the oriental garments presented to me at Algiers had been replaced by others of superior quality, and Blanche had been instructed to brush out all my curls into a pale gold shower under a diamond net. Above this I was supposed to wear an absurdly tiny jewelled cap. The scarlet tinselled slippers were also much too small, and I relieved my feelings by throwing them across the floor.

'Mamzelle,' Blanche protested, 'we've been here three days only, so it's natural that everything is strange.'

'If we'd been here three years it would still be a nightmare. *Three years*—' I stopped suddenly. 'Do you realize *now* what this Sultan is going to mean?'

'Now, Honey, we've been here three whole days without a blink of him, so it's plain he's not going to rush you.'

'And the silence of the place—all so stealthy I could scream.'

'Why, that's those Turks padding around in bedroom slippers—mighty comfortable, nothing to scarify!'

I gazed around with a glazed eye. 'This silence—yet last night that Interpreter said a royal residence holding twenty thousand people! He boasted of its palaces and pleasure-parks, its barracks and its stables—Allah's fortress, he described it. And we are here for life . . . Life, do you hear?'

'Well, Mamzelle, when all's said and done, it's the choicest place we've ever seen. Maybe the gentleman will turn out an elegant surprise too.'

In a low voice I told her, for now I was beyond anger: 'You appall me—he is a heretic, an infidel. We are two Christians buried alive in an empire of heretics.'

Blanche drew herself up, she crossed her hands upon her stomach, and said with dignity: 'Mamzelle, I don't think you're behaving prettily at all. Everybody here has been as polite as can be. I never met the equal of the Turkish officers who met us at the jetty. And all of them, down on their knees five times a day saying their prayers—in the corridors or the garden. As soon as that Voice calls from the tower, down they go, high and low alike, with all the crockery, no matter the inconvenience. Then there's the food—fit for angels. Yes, and hot as hell too. After what we've eaten in that Convent, it's like paradise.'

Bitterly I said: 'No spoons, knives or forks. We might be savages.'

Calmly she nodded. 'Fingers were made before forks. And they always bring the daintiest little napkin with a silver bowl of water—scented too. Don't know what it is about this blessed place, but I feel I could sing.'

I stared at her for a second. 'You're either mad —or totally devoid of imagination.'

'That's right!' and she chuckled. 'Got no imagination to upset me. I've got hope instead. Might have been drowned in Biscay Bay, and here we are—high and dry in luxury!'

Sombrely I said: 'Death might be better than slavery.'

'No, no, Honey. My mother was a slave till your mother bought us out. Wasn't the end—'twas the beginning.'

Suddenly I was ashamed. 'Yes, I must—I *will* take heart. I shall throw myself on the Sultan's mercy. Look at the jewels on this silly little cap—such a rich Emperor cannot grudge us freedom.'

Blanche picked it up and replaced it on my head. 'Mamzelle, you just wear this little cap as if it were a crown, and they'll forget you are a slave. But keep the veil down, for it seems to drive them frantic when you don't. Now, take a peep at that pretty view. Nothing's better than the sea—when you're not afloat.'

'No,' and I groaned despite myself. 'All my courage went with the Dey of Algiers. I'm even afraid of the window now. At any moment a face may appear—'

'A face?' Blanche laughed. 'There's a drop of a hundred feet and more. If the Sultan comes, it won't be by the window!'

'And it won't be by the door,' I reminded her, 'for there's not one in the place—far less a key. It's all part of the nightmare. No privacy.'

But Blanche's patience had given way. 'Mamzelle,' she said sternly, 'you're too bad. Interpreter is never done telling you that as long as your slipper stays outside that red curtain no one will disturb you. I've only to clap my hands when I take it in for them to bring you anything you want. It's as private as a desert island.'

Swiftly I challenged her, once more beside myself with anger: 'Open the curtain!'

Striding to the velvet curtain, Blanche flung it

wide. It revealed a giant Nubian sentry, immobile and fully armed, across the delicate Moorish gate. In one hand he held the whip of hippopotamus hide, symbol of his office as eunuch . . .

My son, this sight, to you who have known it from infancy, is that of the most satisfactory sentry in the world, but to this stranger then, it was a terrifying spectacle.) Yet not to the amazing Blanche:

'Morning, Samson!' she announced cheerfully.

The sentry did not move a muscle.

Ironically I said: 'Company on the desert island! Close the curtain.'

'Looks reliable to me,' and Blanche drew the curtain. 'Just can't think why he never utters. Three days we've been here now.'

In desperation I sprang to my feet. 'I've thought of another plan! Call the Interpreter.'

Blanche wagged a warning finger. 'Mamzelle, just watch your step with that Interpreter. He's the only one that I don't fancy here. He's a Greek, and the Greeks are cunning. I knew a Greek in Martinique and he was as smart as sin. But anyone can see that those Turks are all respectable.'

'*Respectable!* The unspeakable Turk—'

Sharply she interrupted, 'That's the Christian notion—but it won't be healthy here. So, for a change, just you be the cleverest little Honey that ever sweetened quince.' As she moved to the curtain again, she added: 'If I think you're growing dangerous, or somewhat, I'll pipe a little whistle.'

At the curtain she stooped, retrieved a tinselled slipper from behind it, laid it to one side—then clapped her hands twice. There was a slight pause as she held the curtain back, then a few minutes later the Interpreter entered.

He was the only person I could be said to know there, and he always entered with the same stylish aplomb—there is no other word for it. He was a slim and supple gentleman of about thirty years with a sweet smile and cold eyes. He wore a heavily tasselled fez with his Zouave jacket, and embossed trousers. He again made the Turkish salutation—hand to ground, to heart, mouth and forehead, but so airily that deep respect became a graceful gesture—no more.

'Worshipful Lady, today you are happy? Yes? No? Yes? Your sleep has been seraphic? You have accomplished a ravishing toilet? Your broken heart is mended? You are reconciled to your arresting fate in this poor palace, so charmed to accommodate your beauty—yes, no, yes?'

'No,' I retorted with finality, 'but thank you for your courtesy.'

'You have only to name your desire.'

Distinctly I said: 'The French Minister, or Consul to the Sublime Porte.'

'Worshipful Lady, such a personage does not exist.'

'He does, he does,' triumphantly I declared it. 'This morning I remembered. A French Consul was established here by François I in the sixteenth century. In the reign of Soliman the Magnificent. A civilizing influence, the Convent said—'

Alertly Blanche whistled below the unglazed window. The Interpreter paid not the slightest attention to this intrusive bird.

'Worshipful Lady,' he replied, 'since these enlightened emperors departed this life, consuls have fluctuated for decades at a time. Your esteemed country is at present on the worst possible terms with the Ottoman Empire.'

'Merciful heavens,' I exclaimed, 'oh, what am I to do?'

Again Blanche whistled, this time scanning the ceiling for the bird—

'Take comfort, Worshipful Lady. As the gracious gift of the Dey of Algiers, you are now an Ottoman subject. At no time has the Imperial Seraglio come under the jurisdiction of any but the Sultan himself.'

I heard my own helpless gasp, then breathlessly I added: 'I have sent for you to urge another reason for my immediate return to France. I desire only a simple life. I am not worthy of this honour—to become one of your Emperor's wives.'

'Lady, again take comfort. The Sultan has neither wife, nor wives. His Sublime Dignity does not permit himself to enter into any domestic relationship. All here are his slaves. When a woman becomes a mother, she is raised to the rank of Kadine. She has her own sumptuous apartment, her own household compared to which this poor suite may be termed *nothing*. Should she bear a son, she then achieves a palace. A country full of possibility—Yes? No? Yes?'

Faintly I said, 'No, yes, no!'

The Interpreter ignored this negative response. 'Dispose yourself to slumber and enjoyment,' he announced. 'Months may pass before the Sultan deigns to notice your existence. All you may hope for then is a glance from his august eye, due to the importance of a gift from the esteemed Dey of Algiers. Needless to say,' and again he lightly sketched a bow, 'your mature charms may doubtless please as well.'

'My mature charms?' I could not believe my ears.

'At our last interview you confided with pathos that you were twenty years old. A considerable age in a lady—'

Recklessly I interrupted, '*Months* may pass, you say? I cannot bear this, at any age—a prisoner here, far from my home!'

'Ha!' gaily he wagged his forefinger, 'you are

already a good Turk. Old associations—and they are as sentimental as homing pigeons. But I, a Greek, smile at such backward ways. The future is all, is everything . . . And were I an Armenian I should want someone else's future as well! But every elderly lady in the Harem will be enchanted by your nostalgia.'

Stiffly I retorted: 'I am scarcely as old as all that! I too have a spirit of adventure, but to be captured by Corsairs and then find myself in the Sultan's Harem is almost beyond belief.'

'Worshipful Lady, your humility is added virtue. Accept your notable fate with alacrity. Undeniably it is yours. Consider your destiny if captured by the British—doomed to dwell in perpetual fog with a jealous and arrogant people who cannot even cook their own national dish—the cabbage!'

As he spoke we heard a distant flourish on a trumpet, the first time we had known such a commotion there. The Interpreter, startled, raised the red velvet curtain. We heard the warning crack of the hippopotamus whip, and then the eunuch's voice impassively declaring in words that I later learned meant: 'Women withdraw! Women withdraw!'

Over his shoulder the Interpreter hastily told me: 'His Highness himself—I must go!'

But I had run from the divan towards him. 'No, no, don't leave me!'

'His Highness has total command of your language. I am redundant. Adieu—'

As he plunged through the curtain, there came another flourish on the trumpet, at hand this time.

'Oh, Blanche, Blanche!' blindly we clung to each other.

The next minute, as my slipper was no longer outside the door, His Highness the Kisslar Agassi entered with a small retinue. Of pure Nubian descent, his skin was as dark as Egypt's night, and he bore his silver wand of office so regally and was of such majestic appearance in his high hat and rich robes that I at once concluded that he was the Sultan—

Then, still supported by Blanche, I realized that His Highness was bowing benevolently to me. By a supreme effort I recovered myself and swept him a trembling curtsey. In a voice barely above a whisper I said: 'Your Imperial Majesty!'

Graciously this regal personage raised me. 'No, no, His Highness the Kisslar Agassi . . . Master of His Imperial Majesty's Household and Councillor of State. I am at your service, Gentle Lady, now and always.'

These words were spoken in perfect French, with such dignity and sincerity that, in my relief, I took courage. Clasping my hands, I besought him:

'Your Highness, may I speak with you alone?'

'Gentle Lady, I only understand your language. Nevertheless—'

At a sign from him his retinue retired, and he continued to gaze at me with a benign attention which, then and always afterwards, was to set him wholly apart.

'Your Highness,' I began, 'I implore your help! Your kindness restores my confidence—I have been at my wits' end. But now I feel I may speak openly. I can mean nothing to His Imperial Majesty—yet my own life, worth less than a glance to him, is sweet to me. And freedom is all to—to any guest.'

'Gentle Lady, you are more highly esteemed than any guest. You are a gracious gift from the Dey of Algiers himself. A gift cannot be returned, nor yet given away. The situation is of unique delicacy, as one of your refinement will perceive.'

With something like a sob I said, 'Then I must beg an audience of the Sultan and beseech his mercy that I may return home.'

Gravely His Highness said: 'An audience from the Padishah is a favour which crowned heads scarcely solicit.'

'But I have read somewhere that your humblest subject has the right to approach the Sultan once a week—when His Imperial Majesty has prayed at the Mosque. Surely then my tears would melt his heart?'

For the first time the Kisslar Agassi looked alarmed.

'Tears, Gentle Lady? Nothing could produce a worse result. Our Sublime Padishah has the greatest possible aversion to this womanly weakness. So pronounced is this disapproval that tears are officially forbidden at Court. Here no tear ever falls—'

'No tears in Turkey?' I repeated. 'But surely there must be occasions—bereavement, sorrow, fear?'

The Kisslar Agassi smiled. 'Occasions possibly, but never tears! Our Padishah has every virtue, each benevolence, but tears remain taboo.'

'And if—by accident—one fell?'

He laughed. 'The result would be explosive.'

I could not even smile. In desperation I said: 'Then is there no woman at Court who might have pity on me? Perhaps His Imperial Majesty's revered mother? Yes, yes, a mother would have compassion. Oh, I implore you—let me appeal to her!' As I spoke I suddenly remembered that strange sense of reassurance I had had on arrival, and with it came a fey and passionate intuition now. 'Almost I can feel his mother's presence here—a gracious influence, in this very room! She will have pity and protect me. I feel it . . . I *know* it!'

With the utmost gravity he said: 'Gentle Lady, you do not know of what, or of whom you speak. Our Padishah is the ruler of forty million souls and Caliph of two hundred millions more. Throughout the Ottoman Empire one only is enthroned next him in rank. It is she of whom you speak—the Veiled Sultan herself. The Crown of the Veiled Head is the greatest dignity and power attainable by any woman in the world. Even were it possible, none but the Sultan dare approach her—'

I wrung my hands. 'I *know* you are kindness itself. I beseech you to believe me, for I have the strongest conviction also of the Veiled Sultan's compassion. I am certain that she knows of my plight, that she is even now *thinking* of me. I can't explain it, but I feel she is with me now . . . I can sense her with me in this room.'

For a second he was silent. 'Gentle Lady, the Veiled Sultan is dead . . . the Throne of the Veiled Head has been empty for years.'

I passed my hand over my face. 'This is the strangest thing that has ever happened to me . . .' and he led me, dazed, to the divan.

As he seated himself opposite, I was able to say remotely but more calmly, 'If I have distressed you, forgive me.'

Very quietly he said: 'The Empress was a Christian slave—as the mothers of the Sultans have sometimes been.'

'A Christian . . .' I was staggered by his words. 'Was she allowed to see a priest?'

Silently he shook his head.

'But I have heard church bells across this water?'

'A priest is forbidden in any Moslem household. Such would afflict the Faithful. But nobody will interfere with your private devotions. The Empress was devoutness itself. For eleven centuries the tolerance of the Turk has secured the power of the Ottoman Empire'—and he emphasized the next words—'among nine million people of divers races.'

In a low voice I repeated, 'But she had no priest here in all those years—what deprivation, what sacrifice!'

'Ah, Gentle Lady, life without sacrifice ends as mere existence and a stranger to joy. She was known as the Empress of Endless Devotion—and no stranger to joy.'

'No stranger to joy?' Deeply moved, I forgot myself. 'What a revelation to meet you here. You too have the secret, like our Mother Superior at the Convent—' Earnestly I gazed at him. 'But I think you hold more of it because you seem so much happier! Yes, you must belong to the Magi. You are one of the three Wise Kings out of the East who found the Star—' I smiled apologetically, 'more than a human being, a kind of angel.'

The guard stared at me, the courtier and the statesman in him silenced for a second by my involuntary tribute. Then he bowed, 'Gentle Lady, I receive many potentates and powers at the Selamlik, but none have spoken with such grace! Many of our customs may seem strange, but I vow to you that later you will find us as humane as your own people. The civilization of this city goes back to antiquity, as you know. Constantine considered it the capital of the world. Your credentials extol your scholarship. Soon you must visit our library. I shall arrange this.'

'A library?' I was at once alert. 'With pen, paper, and a dictionary I might prepare a petition—in Turkish—for the Sultan?'

'It is a notable conception. Be patient. Not only do I promise that no harm shall come to you, but I will also answer for your happiness here. And in this country a vow is sacred. Now I will say adieu. In a few minutes the Sultan returns from his weekly visit to the Mosque, where he has been in prayer for his people. Today he returns by this entrance. From the lattice you may catch a glimpse of this unique procession. Officers of state will precede and follow him, with the Janissaries as bodyguard. Adieu!'

As he left the room, Blanche dropped the curtain and thrust out the slipper.

'That is a most superior person,' she announced.

But I was still standing stricken after my curtsey to His Highness. 'It is more hopeless than I thought—yet somehow I am sustained. The Kisslar Agassi is a noble being.'

'Mamzelle, those Janissaries? I seem to have heard that name before. Who are they?'

I seated myself on the divan, still in the same

curious calm, my mind full of that remarkable awareness of the Veiled Sultan—an experience that was to set that day forever apart, as in it I had had my first living perception of the celestial world. 'The Janissaries are the shock troops of the East and the terror of Europe.'

'You don't say! Well, now, we should be safe—' she stopped short. Military music could be heard, an overpowering invasion of sound after the somnolence of the past three days. 'My, my, my!' she exclaimed, 'that music certainly beats the band,' and she climbed on to the hassock below the circular window. 'Mother of mercies, what's happening now?'

Blanche was so entranced by the spectacle approaching by avenue and court that she scarcely noticed that I was still rigid on the divan, staring blankly into my prison again.

The room, which had briefly filled with heroic music, was once more as suddenly silent—the light had the thunder-glare known in the Orient about two in the afternoon. There came a bugle call, followed by the harsh clash of soldiers presenting arms—then a triumphant, concerted shout burst from a thousand throats.

'PADISHAH! CHOK YASHA!'

(The Sultan! Let him live forever!)

The next moment I heard the rush of horses' hooves, nearer and nearer . . . louder and louder as the procession flew past our wing, and beyond.

'Quick, quick!' Blanche shouted. 'You never saw such a sight in all your life—the horses, the uniforms, the banners . . . oh, those banners!'

But I remained frozen where I was.

'Mamzelle, Mamzelle, this must be *him* coming now—on a white charger. Oh, what a banner!'

At that instant the assembly's jubilant shout, like gunfire in its exclamatory force, echoed outside from the stone court again, and yet again:

'Padishah! Chok Yasha!'

Involuntarily, I rose to my feet although I still did not face the window—I simply stood blindly, mutely to attention.

'Oh, my blessed lady,' Blanche called breathlessly, 'if only you had seen him! What a miracle, what a miracle. You are saved. There goes a man in a million!'

But I paid not the slightest attention to Blanche's transports from the window, knowing too well the exuberance of that optimist—

As I write, how near and dear is that bygone day. What would I not give now to relive it once again, dreads and all! A distant, sun-struck afternoon set suddenly to music . . . .

## 6. THE THRESHOLD

FOR the remainder of the week its previous sleepy silence settled on my suite of rooms. The stone court outside that wing of the building was again deserted, the garden as solitary as the evening I first entered it. My fear of the Sultan, born of past self-importance, now struck me as absurd, yet for all that I was a prisoner, and although panic had subsided, my misery was still very real. In this heaviness, the reassurance of the Veiled Sultan's presence became a remembrance only.

One gleam of hope absorbed me. The Kisslar Agassi had sent a missive shortly after our meeting, stating that he hoped to arrange my visit to the library in the course of a few days. This seemed to suggest that he too thought my plan of the petition feasible. I brightened. And when the Interpreter next suggested that I 'took a little promenade in the adjoining pleasure-park, where more life was to be seen,' I did so . . . and found a number of visitors sauntering there as decorous as those in any other holiday resort—more so, in fact, for all were veiled.

Together with Blanche I made my way, on another occasion, to the Hammam—but fled on the threshold, intimidated by a bath-house gaiety as frenzied as a parrot-house. Later, with as little success, I ventured by accident into the School of Odalisques. Not only were these girls unveiled but a number, to my astonishment, stood naked on a dais, maintaining languishing postures with insipid smiles. Blanche, who thought that we had stumbled upon some amateur theatrical rehearsal, considered that the circus at Nantes would have afforded the Sultan more amusement.

Next day, seated in the pleasure-park, I found myself for the first time in conversation with another veiled resident. To my astonishment I discovered that this charming woman was a Parisienne. She told me, with a little sigh, that she had awaited the summons to the Alcove for five years. Now, of course, it would never come. She was twenty-two. Yet life here was pleasant enough—as long as one had an interest, a study, or some hobby . . . She advised this strongly, although I had not confided in her.

Thus within a few days I realized conclusively that most of these women would scarcely ever see the Sultan except at a distance, far less be seen by him—that nearly all were there by their own consent, or by that of their relatives, and delighted to be so! Already, with the utmost courtesy, His Highness the Kisslar Agassi had made it plain that as an individual I was of no importance to His Imperial Majesty, except as a gift from the Dey of Algiers.

So, with growing hope and mounting impatience, I clung now to the thought of the petition—and that visit to the library where I might at last prepare it.

Yet, unimportant as I was, a small stone flung into a great lake, ripples had begun to spread unknown to myself—and with comical results.

Long afterwards the Kisslar Agassi told me part of that story—the rest I was finally to hear from the Sultan himself. This then is as it happened . . . .

# 7. THE AUDIENCE CHAMBER

I CAN picture that first droll disturbance so well now, although then I had not seen the Audience Chamber—those massive pillars conjuring vistas which all led to the Sultan's Throne, where cloth-of-gold curtains swept to the vermilion carpet covering the unseen shallow steps of the Imperial divan . . . then soaring to be gathered again into that majestic diadem above—

And to the right of this Veiled Throne that golden duplicate, set farther back, but higher, forming an alcove on its own . . . The second Veiled Throne is, of course, ever slightly shadowed, and at that date a wreath of cypress around its lofty crown lent it the mystery of a shrine. Later, I was to learn that the Veiled Sultan, when alive, was never seen by women of lesser dignity. The ladies of the Seraglio when summoned only glimpsed this flight of broad steps covered with crimson which led to the lattice-screen behind the golden curtain. A perpetual social isolation was then considered fitting for the greatest Queen of the Orient—the Empress of Byzantium.

This particular spring day was already warm as June, and to the right, overlooked by the Empress's hidden throne, lay the sea beyond her balcony-gardens, where once she had heard the gentle splashing of waves ....

Two courtiers stood as usual to attention on either side of the centre throne. In front of the second throne there was the customary third courtier, remote in its shadow, with bowed head, his hands clasped on the hilt of his sword, its blade resting on the ground.

This afternoon other courtiers were sparsely grouped, for the day's event was not a formal reception, but as ever in the background were ranged the giant deaf-mute Nubian slaves who remain immovable as the pillars themselves. Yet the prevailing impression on an informal occasion was always one of light, calm, and privacy—perhaps because His Highness the Kisslar Agassi stood at the post of honour outside the Veiled Throne, at the Sultan's right hand, amiably observing the two persons about to be received in audience today.

Prince Mustapha, the Sultan's only son, aged twelve, a delicate boy, faced the throne, side by side with his mother. The Persian Kadine, unveiled now because the Sultan was imminent, was a dark, sprightly woman who sometimes suggested a jewelled bird, for her draperies were often a mosaic of brilliant colours in which peacock shades prevailed.

The black bar of her eyebrows was not so marked as in a Turkish lady, but her manner was sharper, although, like a second thought, she had a soft laugh that other women came to dread—a little gurgle, not quite a titter. Part Persian, part Armenian, energy as endless as her ambition had endowed her with a sense of complete adequacy. As I later discovered, her attitude to her son, from start to finish, was a dangerous mingling of exasperation, compassion and determination. His future was, naturally, her obsession . . . .

Today, as they waited, a fanfare sounded and the courtiers on either side of the throne swept back the lofty gold curtains. This revealed that further diaphanous veil which invariably gives an enchanting mystery to the vivid presence of the seated Sultan. He could be seen, but only with the wayward clarity of an image glimpsed in water. At this date all that the highest European ambassadors ever saw—and when on their knees—was the imperial hand through the outer gold curtain. Fantastic as this seems to us today, a potentate might be allowed to kiss it, but as a rule the Sultan's scarf was extended for this purpose.

But that afternoon through the transparent ivory veil known only to the Seraglio it could be seen that the Sultan was an impressive personality with the spare figure of a notable polo-player, although his vigilant eye could only be surmised. Yet there were glimpses of his austere features, and no doubt whatsoever of his ironic humour! His gestures, which were as incisive as they were slight, came from his hands and wrists alone, and conveyed the effect of an active idol. In this man the natural dignity of the Turk had become an epitome of elegance.

As the fanfare ended, the Sultan extended his hand through the transparent veil, and Mustapha, who had made the Turkish salutation with, finally, both hands folded upon the stomach, Persian fashion, to prove no weapon is carried, advanced, knelt, and kissed the hand.

The Sultan's voice was invariably as expressionless as his face, and he now remarked: 'We are informed that at sunset your Birthday returns with the new day. Twelve is an age with its own problems. What will comfort you on this occasion?'

Nervously the boy said: 'Sire, an Arab charger.'

'Since first you could speak, you have made this request. Had it been granted each time, you would now have a sizable stable.'

Swiftly the Persian Kadine said, 'Sire, he knows only too well that on horse-back he lacks confidence. He is most anxious to excel.'

'Then let him learn to laugh first! Off with you, boy, to the lake. His Highness will show you there a new row-boat, built for one passenger. Escape upon it as often as you can.'

The boy in his relief gave a jump of delight and ran to the Kisslar Agassi.

'*Mustapha!*' his mother exclaimed, and the little prince instantly returned to make his forgotten bow to the Sultan, and then vanished hand in hand with the elderly doyen.

'Why is Mustapha so nervous?' the expressionless voice inquired.

'Sire, he is enchanted to be in your presence!'

'He is biting his nails.'

The Persian Kadine was astonished. 'I have never seen him do so.'

'His nails are bitten to the quick.' The Sultan smiled slightly—'A Persian kitten should have all its claws!' And on a gesture from him, the assembly withdrew but for the two courtiers standing by the Throne, and the third with bowed head before the Throne of the Veiled Empress. Now there only remained the giant Nubian deaf-mute slaves standing to attention in the background. To the Persian Kadine the Sultan said:

'Be seated.'

Gracefully she subsided on a cushion before him.

'Now,' he announced, 'let Us have the latest news.'

Merrily she inquired: 'From the sublime, Sire, to the mundane?'

'In that order—then laughter has the last word.'

'Rumour persists that our Lord of Two Continents and Two Seas continues to visit Stamboul incognito. This gives rise to anxiety among the Faithful for the Sacred Person. The Janissaries,' and she paused for a second to give emphasis, 'are suspicious and displeased. They are, after all, the Imperial Bodyguard.'

'Such steps on the part of the Padishah,' the lifeless voice replied, 'belong to the realm of fantasy, or its guilty conscience. The Imperial Secret Service surpasses any in Europe or the East—its Greek agents are unequalled. Continue.'

'Certain merchants are murmuring also at the decrease in Court festivities and a general curtailment in expenditure—'

Dryly the Sultan interrupted. 'The diamond merchants need scarcely complain. Since the death of the Empress, the Seraglio's expenditure on diamonds has mounted like the sins of commission and omission combined. Proceed.'

With a sympathetic shake of her head the Kadine said: 'It is also whispered that Allah's Shadow upon Earth seldom irradiates his Court. It is also feared that our enemy Russia will suspect a lack of vitality in our economy from this absence of ceremonial occasion. Sire, I too am uneasy.'

'Why?'

'History has repeatedly shown that it is sometimes needful to keep an eye on the Watchman, Sire. But if such visits to Stamboul, incognito, exist, Mustapha is but twelve. Should danger overtake Your Imperial Majesty—'

'A novel idea that We should safeguard Ourself until Mustapha takes Our size in slippers!'

'Sire, it would be presumption to suggest that the Sultan guards himself for my sake.'

'You have not always been so faint-hearted.'

With dignity she replied: 'In the past this heart was sustained by the Imperial favour, and so could brave the Sublime Displeasure. But two years have passed without a single summons to the Imperial Alcove—I can now only plead as Mustapha's mother.'

Impassively the Sultan said: 'Then as Mustapha's mother, a word of advice: be more discreet in those letters to your uncle. Powerful as his position is with the Janissaries, he is not yet all-powerful in that militia.'

'Your Imperial Majesty is well aware *why* I have written him from time to time—that I might keep a finger on the Empire's only danger-pulse, that same militia!'

'Yet from a note enclosed *with* your last letter, it seems that both you and your uncle share a belief that the Sultan's faithful Bulgaria is a menace?'

Fleetly she said: 'In our anxiety to protect your Imperial Majesty, I freely admit that my uncle has become suspicious, and possibly a little jealous of the Bulgarian influence.'

Coldly he replied: 'We would answer for Bulgaria's integrity with Our own. But are *you* no longer happy here—have you too become suspicious, jealous?'

'Suspicious, jealous? Sire, you have made me the happiest woman on earth. Your son is the crown of my life. It is true that I have long recognized your Library as a most dangerous rival. But how can mortal woman hope to prevail among the immortals?'

For a second he raised his finger-tips in her direction with a phantom kiss. 'You are a charmer, and We are still delighted to be spellbound. Having exhausted matters relating to the Sublime, let Us now enjoy the mundane. What is the latest among the twenty thousand of the Seraglio? The Harem invariably knows more about the Selamlik than any man there.'

With her roguish little laugh she told him. 'Sire, the latest excitement has been in the Harem itself. A newcomer among the odalisques has set the cat among the pigeons with her outlandish behaviour.'

'What! Not another of these ladies to support? Our wretched country will be ruined.'

'She is a French woman—a gift from the Dey of Algiers.'

'Ah, a political consideration. More expense.'

'Sire, I have a favour to ask, but knowing your generosity, I hesitate to trespass even for a trifle.'

'What is this bagatelle?'

'Sire, as is known to you, the study of languages is my chief hobby—'

He interrupted, with a slight inclination of his head; 'You first delighted Us on paper. Your love-letters were poems. No other woman has that gift today.'

'Your Imperial Majesty is most gracious. I am anxious to improve my French, and shall be happy if this newcomer might be added to my household.'

'Do you wish to give Our worthy Kisslar Agassi a seizure? He runs this Household. The Sultan merely attends to the Empire—a much less exacting task.'

The Kadine gurgled tolerantly: 'Then I have lost my French tuition! Sire, it is quite impossible for the Kisslar Agassi to do me *any* favour. I am that remarkable man's one and only prejudice.'

'A gift from the Dey of Algiers is not a matter of prejudice but of protocol.'

'But of course! And the odalisque herself might prove a mixed blessing. They say her sobs at night can be heard across the court.'

'Why does the creature weep?'

'Some sort of hysteria. But as Your Sublime Majesty has often said: there is nothing so tedious as a tearful woman.'

Enigmatically the Sultan observed: 'We have ever preferred cheerful sinners.'

'They say the poor thing's pallor is pitiful. But one should sympathize. She is probably consumptive—

in France it always rains. Yes, Sire, it is better, after all, that she is not in contact with Mustapha.'

'You have a genius for alleviation. Let Us hope the lady will recover her health in this congenial air.'

'Yet, Sire, she has already made it much less congenial. At the odalisques' School of Charm she has given deep offence by laughter at the other ladies when in graceful and alluring postures. A pantomime, she described it, which they now understand to mean a feast of absurdities!'

'A view We too have sometimes shared—yet courtesy is imperative.'

'Alas, Sire,' and the Kadine gave an indulgent shrug, 'the Franks are essentially parvenu. This infidel, for one, declines to please. She alone is enough, and without blandishment. As lifeless as a wax peach or a picture on the bath-house wall. That is what the Harem have already named her: Naksh—a picture of beauty. The ladies are nothing if not good-natured there, for I hear that her eyes are as pink as a ferret's with weeping.'

Imperceptibly the Sultan smiled. 'A beauty with the pink eyes of a ferret—you excite curiosity! And you never fail to amuse. Now We will refresh Ourself with cheerful thoughts of your presence—in absence.' Soundlessly, he clapped his hands once.

The Kisslar Agassi, entering on the left, courteously bowed the Persian Kadine out. On his return he found that the Sultan had signalled to one of the two courtiers beside him and was now smoking a cigarette. His face and voice were no longer inscrutable; he looked and sounded both weary and impatient:

'She did not blink an eye-lash over the Janissary note.'

Soothingly the Kisslar Agassi said: 'She is much too intelligent to make the same mistake again. I think the matter may be dismissed.'

'Had the Empress been alive, this absurd audience would never have taken place today.' Impatiently he added, 'Well, now that Our minor headache is dismissed, what of the major malady?'

'Sire, I am happy to report that the trouble at the barracks is settled. Jealousy had again been fomented, but I am not certain that the Persian Kadine's uncle was responsible. The Janissaries are the spoiled children of the Empire. Their every claim is buttressed by precedent. But one must go warily with them—they have been a law unto themselves for generations. Too long! Superiority now is less their due than their tradition.'

Grimly the Sultan said: 'We shall solve that difficulty yet for the Empire—if it kills Us. Rome had precisely the same problem with the Praetorian cohorts—as Constantine knew to his cost!'

'Sire, you are driving yourself too hard.'

'No,' the Sultan retorted sardonically. 'Merely

poet's licence, as where Nizami says: *I am like a dead body with the soul of a man, But not journeying with the caravan, or one of its company.'*

The Kisslar Agassi shook his head. 'Your Imperial Majesty is with your secretaries from dawn till noon. When the Divan is in session you are with your Ministers till nightfall. And after dining, you again resume your portfolio.'

'Work never killed yet.'

'Sire, you have lost interest in life, so the work has become an exhaustion.'

The Sultan gave a soundless laugh. 'High treason! Not another man in the Empire would have the courage to state that—nor the wit to perceive it. Yes, We now find all affairs of state too predictable. We know the men and their reactions by rote. Less skill is needed in that manipulation than in a game of chess. As for the various Ambassadors behind the Lattice, We can now detect the thoughts of the Russian fox a split second before he opens his mouth.'

The Kisslar Agassi was startled. 'You know the words, Sire, before he utters them? Does this mean that Your Imperial Majesty now has the Other Sight—the vision of both worlds?'

'Nothing of the sort. It is observation brought to an unusual pitch, coupled with the fact that each man does not alter within his own range. He has his individual gamut—then repetition quenches him.

Some have a wider range than others, but all are subject to that personal limitation which declares them. You know this well, for you are the most intelligent man at Court.'

The Kisslar Agassi laughed, amused, but the Sultan added: 'Yes, there is more to *your* tune than to most, but even yours is disappointing. You are, alas, incorrigibly benevolent, and so your vital energy—the one element that interests your Padishah—is dissipated on fallible human nature.'

Still laughing, the Kisslar Agassi remarked: 'But, Sire, at least I am happy in my work!'

The Sultan regarded him ironically. 'You have achieved a remarkable position, and the jealousy of others keeps you alert. We are the Caliph, and short of assassination will remain supreme, with very little trouble to Ourself. True, We have endless exercise in the administration of the Empire, but as you have guessed—it is not enough.'

'There is too much harassment. Your Imperial Majesty has taken more burdens on your shoulders than any Padishah of the past.'

'These We find essential—but your galas and festivities bore Us to extinction, so be warned! Leave your Sultan to his work. There at least he can forget in exhaustion that he too cannot escape the penalty of his limitation—' With a satirical smile he held up a monitory finger, 'His range of *one*—which is, alas, a final note!'

'Sire, it has been said that our final note cannot be struck—beyond the octave, it escapes in light!'

The Sultan was silent for a second. 'A pleasing fancy! And light is certainly the emblem of Our country.' He shrugged pleasantly, 'Well, perhaps within the isolation of the Crescent your Sultan may yet find his star.'

The Kisslar Agassi shook his head reminiscently. 'That star again! Sire, recently a newcomer to the Seraglio invoked it for me. Infidels themselves cling to the sacred symbol. I refer to the odalisque sent by the Dey of Algiers—direct from the French Convent.'

The Sultan frowned. 'The Dey is too shrewd to ship any female so far without sound reason. What is behind this gift?'

'Your Imperial Majesty, she is a French gentlewoman, captured at sea by his Corsairs. He has sent her on a ship of state, attired like Sheba, for she is peerlessly beautiful.'

'They are all peerlessly beautiful. But the Dey is no fool. There must be another reason for this expenditure. Has he dispatched her credentials?'

'Yes, Sire, and I have studied these, which include scholastic reports. The war between England and France delayed her at the Convent. She is now twenty years of age.'

'As old as that? Her significance can only be political.'

'Sire, she comes of Norman stock, and from the age of thirteen has been immured in this Convent at Nantes. Such girls mature later than those of the south and east. Her school reports state that she is highly intelligent, with a marked proficiency in languages. I tend to think that her gift for languages has influenced the Dey—and the fact that she is also musical.'

'In which subjects is she weak?'

Regretfully the Kisslar Agassi admitted: 'History and arithmetic.'

'Every French woman can count in her sleep. The Convent's method has been defective. See that she has an efficient teacher at once. Include a tutor on history—' he added dryly, 'start at the Crusades.'

'Sire it is as much as we can do at present to persuade her to smile. Tuition will be fruitless until she feels more at home.'

'At home! After eight years in a cheerless convent where the nuns sleep on boards and to bathe—' the Sultan shuddered, 'is forbidden—why! she is now in paradise. Moreover, she has escaped from France where both rain and mistral prevail. Domestically and geographically she has bettered her lot without raising a finger. Such destinies compel attention. Why is she not on her knees to Allah for this deliverance?'

'Assuredly, Sire! Yet the circumstances in which this particular female arrived in our earthly paradise are undoubtedly a trifle unusual. She is just a little nervous—possibly afraid.'

'Of what?' the Sultan said flatly.

'Sire, the wretched Franks are so accustomed to a dissolute monarchy that terror and suspicion are every convent-girl's reaction to a life at Court. Then, too, she is somewhat indisposed after her long sea voyage—a touch of *mal de mer*.'

'You venerable humbug! We have been called many things in Our time, but never before *mal de mer*. Set the poor thing's mind at rest by defining the rigorous etiquette of the Imperial Court. Specify that in *any* Turkish household every concubine is legally safeguarded and her future secure. Confirm that no country in the world protects its women as We do. Then give her all she wants, within reason. And now enough of such trifles—' he stretched out his hand for a portfolio of State papers.

'Sire, she has only asked me for one thing.'

The Sultan looked up impatiently. 'This ferret with the pink eyes has become a bore. What is the matter with you today, Balthazar? Give her whatever it is.'

Quietly the Kisslar Agassi said, 'She has asked for a Turkish dictionary, Sire. Despite her Interpreter.'

'A Turkish dictionary?' The Sultan was momentarily arrested. 'Then We were right. We cannot be too careful. What is the Dey playing at?'

The Kisslar Agassi lowered his gaze. 'Sire, I have

arranged for her to visit the Library tomorrow. She states that she wishes to submit some request to the Padishah . . . eventually, of course, and at His Sublime Pleasure—but in His Own Language.'

'A ruse of course to attract Our attention. But quite a clever one—' the Sultan stared at the Kisslar Agassi for a moment. 'She probably speaks Turkish as well as you do. We would put nothing past the Dey! Send her to the Nizami Library tomorrow at an hour We shall later appoint—unaccompanied.'

'The Nizami Library, Sire?' the Kisslar Agassi was astonished.

'Yes, but see that she comes veiled—it is not an Audience. We will solve this conundrum in Our own way. Five minutes should do it—' he opened the portfolio. 'You may go, Balthazar.'

Years later the Kisslar Agassi related that as he turned to go, he found it difficult to hide a smile.

Scarcely had he taken two steps than the Sultan spoke again:

'Give her no explanation, of course. Simply state that the Chief Librarian will be there to help her—' acidly he added, '*with* a Turkish dictionary!'

# 8. THE NIZAMI LIBRARY

I DRESSED with unusual care for my visit to the library. It was my first formal appearance in public there, and I pictured a large hall lined with books—possibly a number of sages in attendance, and perhaps a good many students veiled like myself. Besides, my spirits had risen, the petition might prove the solution—and now the opportunity to prepare it had come. So, with genuine satisfaction I arranged my pale-green draperies and allowed Blanche to settle the tiny violet cap more securely on my ash-gold hair, already shimmering beneath its diamond net. Bidding me good luck during this hour's absence, she declared that under this costly dew I looked like a spring flower sparkling!

With a guide on either side, I was somewhat surprised by the length of time it took to reach the Library—through endless corridors and each empty but for its sentinels. Eventually, I was bowed into an empty chamber alone, its white arched recesses housing what was obviously a collection of valuable books and manuscripts.

As I walked forward I perceived that a remarkable feature of this interior was that the floor was also of milky satin-wood. I passed along a series of arched recesses, and by the silence seemed to be the only person present. Then these white aisles ended in a square white chamber with an alcove lined with imperial yellow, in front of which was an elaborately carved ivory lectern. This Chinese-yellow alcove, which concealed a small yellow divan, and two remote window-arches framing the intense blue sky, were the only notes of colour in an interior of muted white and ivory—for, I discovered, the other divan at right angles to the lectern was also white. No carpet was laid on the gleaming floor and I thought it the most lovely chamber I had ever seen. But I was puzzled by its deserted appearance—not a slave to be seen. . .

As I hesitated in my archway, a man stepped forward, in profile, from the Chinese-yellow alcove and, without apparently seeing me, took up his position at the lectern, where he continued to study a manuscript. He was dressed completely in white—turban, tunic, trousers, slippers—only his sash had a gold fringe, and he wore one heavy signet ring. His features were pale, keenly cut, somewhat forbidding, but from the elegance and simplicity of his attire he was obviously the presiding genius of the place.

As I eyed him cautiously above my yashmak, he became aware of me. Once again I forgot the

Turkish salutation, and instead made my involuntary curtsey, my diaphanous draperies presenting the effect of a butterfly spreading, then folding, and finally lowering its wings.

'Good afternoon, sir,' I said in French. 'I am told that you speak my language and will be kind enough to help me.'

Somewhat surprisingly, he was silent for a moment. Then he spoke. 'We are pleased to do what we can to help you. You have only to express your wish. The Sultan has here a notable collection of books and manuscripts, in all languages.'

I felt a slight alarm. 'There is no chance of His Imperial Majesty arriving, I hope—I must not trespass.'

'Rest assured. You are now alone with the Chief Librarian and will remain so.'

With fervour I said: 'There are some honours that intimidate—how kind of you to understand! I spend my life here placing my slipper outside my room to ensure privacy. Or rather Blanche does.'

'That will certainly not be necessary in the Nizami Library. Who, or what is Blanche?'

The Librarian had a stately, somewhat elderly manner that I found reassuring—older than his years. 'Blanche is my Negress maid,' I confided. 'She has been with me since childhood. She too was captured by those dreadful Corsairs. Now we are prisoners here.'

'As an honoured guest, are you not happy?'

Earnestly I said: 'No, I am not—although it is only fair to add that Blanche is delighted with everything.'

'We fail to see the importance of Blanche's point of view. Will you not be seated?'

'Thank you, but I am always more intelligent if I stand—the divan is a trifle low. Blanche's point of view is most important. I am not receiving from her the moral support I need.'

'Do you not find our country beautiful, this poor palace comfortable?'

'Most beautiful, most comfortable—the entrance by the Golden Horn is like the entrance to some celestial city, and the palace is a dream of delight—but without freedom I cannot live.'

The librarian shook his head. 'You are doomed in any case. Greed will undoubtedly be your downfall.'

'Greed?' I was astounded.

'Every urgent desire is a shackle. Happy is she who can live within her own egg-shell, and find in its tracery of veins rivers of delight that bear her to the kingdom of the mind.'

I gazed at him, spellbound. 'How very strange. You remind me of my Mother Superior. She too spoke of freedom as you do.'

'Strange indeed to resemble your maternal parent. Without doubt this is the most curious tribute we have yet received.'

'Forgive me,' I said hurriedly. 'As Mother Superior of the Convent she would say that all comparisons are odious! The Convent always called a spade a spade. I am too impulsive.'

He bowed briefly. 'It is the nature of the fountain to foam and fall.'

'Is that how I strike you? Yes, at present I *am* too urgent, but at any moment we may be interrupted'—I looked round quickly—'and this makes me nervous, for you are almost my last hope.'

'Urgency need not trouble you. We shall not be interrupted.'

But I glanced round again. 'How can you be so sure? His Highness the Kisslar Agassi might come, or some other dignitary. To begin my story and then break off might leave you with a wrong impression.'

'Reluctant Guest,' he said in the same impassive way, 'we have all the time there is. Continue to reveal your impassioned thoughts. Your energy of expression is an astonishment.'

'Now you are laughing at me? At my unhappy state?'

'Suspicion is the freak sister of fear. We shall not be interrupted. Here the Chief Librarian rules supreme. The tradition of local self-government in Turkey is very old and very strong.'

Encouraged, I drew nearer the lectern and stood immediately below him. Lowering my voice, I said:

'You actually enjoy a position of control here? Then, if my petition to the Sultan fails, you yourself might—might be able to aid me privately?'

He gave a slight bow. 'Anything that can be done, shall be done—within reason.'

I clasped my hands, 'Oh, do not be too reasonable!' and I gave a half-sob. 'I am almost in despair—'

Sharply he said, 'But one tear here and I might lose my post—or my head!'

With another tearful sniff I said, 'Then I too must call a spade a spade,' and I looked round hurriedly again. 'Can I trust you?'

'With what?' he said flatly.

'My life,' I said in a low, and I think impressive, voice.

'It is as safe as my own—here.'

'I scarcely know how to begin,' and again I hesitated. 'The Chief Librarian might take fright and betray me.'

'And again he might not.'

'Then if my petition to the Sultan for freedom fails, might I—may I count on you?'

'To return his gift to the Dey of Algiers?'

'No, no!' I cried alarmed. 'I am better here than there—that terrible man! Oh, if you only knew what I have suffered since he captured me!'

'What have you suffered?' the Librarian inquired. 'Be explicit.'

'Agonies of suspense,' and again I lowered my voice. 'Yet I do not want to commit suicide unless it is essential. On arrival I thought of knocking out all my front teeth, in the hope that the Sultan would be so revolted by my appearance that I should be ordered from his sight forever. But Blanche feared that with this plan, *her* head might roll in the dust.'

Calmly the Librarian said: 'Our Sultan is nothing if not just. Your fraudulent head would have been more likely to fall.'

Despairingly I begged him: 'Then what can I do if the petition fails? It will have to be a wholly exceptional man, one who does not put his own interests first, who helps me.'

'It will indeed,' he replied somewhat grimly.

'To ask such a sacrifice of a stranger would be a great deal, I know.'

'Of anyone it would be more than that. But let us take your numerous desires in their order. First, we understand, you wish a Turkish dictionary?'

'No,' I said mournfully. 'I have now decided against the Turkish dictionary. It would take too long. Instead, I shall tell *you* what I want to say in the petition, and you will perhaps be kind enough to put it into Turkish. I will then copy it out in my own writing. The Sultan is bound to be touched by an appeal from a foreigner in his own language.'

'You think so?'

'Yes.' I glanced at the white divan which stood at right angles to the yellow alcove and its divan. 'I think I will sit down after all.' Politely I added: 'Pray don't hesitate to sit down too—'

But the Chief Librarian remained standing and, as I settled on the white divan, I added: 'The Sultan may also be moved by the fact that I have copied out the petition myself.'

'On the contrary, the Sultan tends to be irritated by an uncertain script.' The Librarian's manner was somewhat stiff at times, but always courteous, and with growing confidence I now realized that he was possibly a shy man.

'My script will be clear,' I assured him. 'It is not to be expected that it should be as perfect as yours, or his—' and I gave him a kindly little bow, for of course no smile of encouragement could be seen behind my tiresome veil. 'But although the petition must be politeness itself, sir, it must also be firm. Instinctively I feel that if I am to get away, it will be now or never. Oh, if you only knew how I long for my home at Martinique! To hear you speak my language means everything to me—despite your accent.'

Austerely he said; 'What is the matter with my accent?'

Indulgently I admitted: 'It is Marseillaise—not perhaps the most beautiful in France, but today it is music in my ears.'

'What is the matter with the accent of Marseilles?'

'Nothing, nothing!' I said hastily. 'It twangs like a guitar—in the wrong places, as a Marseillaise accent should. Don't think I'm not enjoying it. I simply did not expect it here. His Highness the Kisslar Agassi's is Parisian.'

'Ha! It is, is it?'

Again I smiled kindly. 'Yes, you have had a very different tutor! But *your* fluency is greater—indeed it is remarkable. At times you tend to be a little shy of the personal pronoun—but with practice this too will come right!'

As the Chief Librarian did not at once reply, but continued to stare at me somewhat stonily, I added sympathetically: 'Please do not hesitate to correct *me* as we go along.'

The Chief Librarian seated himself for the first time—somewhat suddenly. 'Assuredly I shall not fail to do so!'

'There!' I cried triumphantly, 'you've got your personal pronoun right at last. Practice makes perfect.'

Abruptly he replied: 'To return to your petition: three versions in different degrees of firmness will be drawn up—and later sent to your chamber for your approval.'

'How kind you are—you seem to understand intuitively. . . . Which reminds me—in drawing up the petition I wish only one of the Sultan's titles used.'

'It is the custom to give our Sublime Padishah *all* his titles—indeed, imperative when a favour is desired.'

'No,' I was resolute. 'One title will make my petition more arresting still. I have given this much thought. I shall call him simply *Allah's Shadow upon Earth*, for this will remind him forcibly that he has a duty to me too—the stranger within his gates. Oh, sir,' I leaned forward fervently, 'make the petition as moving as you can! If you only knew how I yearn for my own people. Think what *you* would feel if you were suddenly parted from your nearest and dearest.'

Somewhat tartly he replied: 'I would accept that fate quite calmly—with, possibly, a degree of relief.'

I was aghast, for he appeared to be quite sincere. 'But how heartless—and you seem so kind. There must be something wrong. Are you—married?'

'Married!' he expostulated.

'Yes, have you a wife—or . . . wives?'

'I have neither wife nor wives.'

'But surely you must care for someone. Think of your parents.'

Briefly he said, 'Both are in paradise.'

I began to understand him a little better. 'Oh, dear me . . . I'm sorry . . . how very sad.'

'On the contrary. With the Faithful, paradise is bliss.'

Hurriedly I remembered. 'Yes, of course—and this explains your detachment. You are possibly one of those who live for their work?'

'More or less,' he agreed—and his expression was now so much less staid than his manner that I realized my effect on him was one of reassurance. With a gesture I indicated the library. 'You probably see very few people here?'

'Very few.'

I nodded. 'It is certainly a wonderful library, but I can't believe that *anyone* will be allowed to go through life loving books instead of people. That's too easy. You have probably been shut up here too long—away from people and affairs—' I sighed suddenly. 'Perhaps we're both prisoners in a different way. My parents too are in paradise. All this should give you a fellow-feeling for me.'

'What precisely is a fellow-feeling?'

'Sympathy. Should the petition fail, you might even find it in your heart to help me escape?' Again I leaned forward urgently. 'Oh, don't invite reason again! Try to put yourself in my place. Think what it means to me to know that I have enough jewels on my head at this moment to pay for my passage to Martinique—and to reward anyone suitable who helped me.'

Cautiously he said, 'There would scarcely be enough on that fez to reward the Kisslar Agassi for connivance in your escape.'

Sorrowfully I said, 'A kingdom would not be enough for him. I am not a fool. His Highness is a being apart. He has one foot in heaven already and so'—I caught my breath—'is lost for practical purposes.'

'Despite my sheltered life,' he remarked, 'it seems you do not think that I have one foot in heaven.'

Too late,I perceived my mistake. Apologetically I said: 'Well, you are younger, of course, so it would scarcely be natural if you had. But that does not mean you would not be capable of sacrifice. To help a foreigner, and—and—'

'A stranger within the gates?'

'Yes—might mean quite a big sacrifice.'

'It would indeed—if you intend me to betray my Sublime Master, the Sultan, by depriving him of the gift of the Dey of Algiers.'

'No, no—I mean less than nothing to the Sultan. He has countless odalisques whom he never sees. I only ask you to help the homesick, to release the prisoner.'

'But what oppresses you here? Have you not every freedom in this not unpleasing place?'

'To be a slave is not freedom.'

'Reluctant Guest,' he said firmly, 'we are all prisoners of destiny. You are in such haste to escape your present fate that you have not paused to consider its advantages.'

'I am a French woman,' I insisted.

'French women too are subject to the vagaries of time and place.'

'But not as slaves.'

He shrugged. 'This aversion must be a national—or perhaps a provincial peculiarity of yours. Our Sublime Padishah regards *his* title of Slave as possibly his most exalted.'

I was amazed. 'His title of Slave?'

'As Padishah he is Father of all the Sovereigns of earth; he is likewise Pontiff of Mussulmans; Refuge of the World; Lord of Two Continents and Two Seas; Servant of Two Holy Cities; but his final title is the Son of a Slave. As the divine representative of Mahomet and the father of his people, should he not be exalted? But as the son of a slave mother should he not also be humble?'

In an awed voice I said, 'That is truly noble.' Then suddenly I realized: 'Dear heaven, less and less is he likely to sympathize with me.'

'Distracted Guest, do you refer to the Padishah or my miserable self?'

'To both.' I buried my face in my hands. 'To think that I shall never see Joséphine again!'

'Who is Joséphine?'

'My cousin,' with an effort I controlled my tears. 'We were brought up together. I love her more than a sister. And her two children—never to know them more!'

'Between females, friendship is an extravagance.

You will yet love in reality, and if Allah decrees, have your own children.'

Coldly I said: 'It is not the same.'

'It is better.'

'And my poor guardian,' I exclaimed indignantly, 'whom I have not seen since I was a child—what about *his* feelings? He will be distracted—thinking me dead . . . or worse!'

'This guardian—how old is he?'

Sorrowfully I said, 'At least sixty, poor man.'

'It is too old,' the Librarian declared. 'You are better here.'

Shocked, I reproved him: 'It is not too old to feel. He will be heart-broken. I picture him, week after week at the jetty, watching every ship.'

'At sixty he will recover. By that age one has learned acceptance. If not, he is better dead.'

With horror I stared at the Chief Librarian. 'What a callous statement! Living alone here, you do not know the first thing about human nature—*nor* the last.'

But he merely said: 'Didactic One, be good enough to enlighten me.'

'The first and last thing in human nature is the heart. We cannot choose whom we will love. If we *could* choose—' I paused.

'Indeed, yes, if we could choose?'

Soberly I said, 'We would surely all choose God—and be at peace.'

'Reluctant Guest, that observation is sound.'

But I shook my head. 'It has been forced upon me. At the Convent, for a time, I dreamt I might become a nun, but the love of the world outside the window was too much for me. I pined for freedom. Had I taken the veil there, I would not be under this one now.'

'That observation is also undeniable.'

I gave a sigh. 'Life is quite terrifying when you consider it.'

'Not so,' he announced in his dogmatic way. 'On consideration it becomes a parable to enlighten.'

Annoyance got the better of me. 'As the parable itself, I find it *much* too near the bone! But you, who live by rule and reason, cannot understand. Your world is a library!'

'Let me undeceive you there. This hermit without a heart has also had his tender attachments.'

Reproachfully I told him: 'They do not seem to have made much impression on you.'

For the first time he folded his hands and gazed absently into space. 'The conviction persisted that I was not loved for myself alone.'

I was astonished. 'But why? What else have you to offer?'

Without a moment's hesitation he replied: 'My not inconsiderable savings.'

It was I who paused for a second. 'For such a pleasant person,' I told him, 'forgive me if I say it—

you too have rather a suspicious nature. There is no reason why any of these—these attachments should not have valued you for yourself alone.'

'You think so?'

'I do indeed,' I said kindly. 'It is a mistake to underestimate yourself. *This* may have made you harder than you are. You have a most—yes, a most impressive appearance. You have nothing to fear there.'

'That is your view?'

'It undoubtedly is. Your manner is perhaps a little brusque—but you convey integrity. To a woman this means much. I feel certain, for instance, that you will not betray my confidence.'

'Where you are concerned,' he bowed, 'the Chief Librarian is a closed book.'

'Thank you,' I said gratefully, 'thank you from the heart. And I hope that you will yet find happiness with one—or other—of your attachments.'

'I thank you—from such heart as I possess. Yet I scarcely think it likely.'

'But why not?' Our conversation had become increasingly effortless, since I had first perceived his essentially shy nature.

'Because I have never yet carried any woman's slipper in my bosom to the Divan—to our State Council.'

Puzzled, I asked: 'Is that a Turkish custom?'

'An extremely rare one.'

'A slipper in the bosom—what does it mean?'

'Infatuation,' he said grimly.

'But a very pretty compliment,' I smiled. 'I had no idea that the Turkish nature had such tender ideas.'

'So far it has not been one of mine. Reluctant Guest, would it embarrass you if I, in my brusque way, asked you to remove your veil?'

'Not in the least,' I said heartily. 'I feel muffled behind it. Also Blanche says I tend to shout behind it. But those in authority here grow quite frantic if I remove it. Clearly, they attach importance to it—so if you will forgive me, I shall keep it on. His Highness told me to come veiled.'

'His jurisdiction does not apply in this library.'

Soothingly I said, 'I realize that—or you would not have made the request. Yet, as he is much older than you, it will be kinder to defer to him on this trifle.'

'A pity—I have the ability to tell a person's future from his face.'

Eagerly I looked up. 'I know that Eastern people can read the stars—but I did not know that any had this other gift. It *is* a pity that I must not remove the veil.'

Crisply he said: 'It is indeed. The structure of the face and skull tell much to the instructed. Nevertheless, if you will take up your stance at the lectern here, I shall tell you what I can from your eyes.' In a business-like way he added: 'I have already noticed a marked peculiarity in your brows.'

Alarmed, I exclaimed: 'They are entirely normal—' but I almost ran to the lectern. 'Turkish ladies add black bars to theirs—but apart from this I'm sure there is nothing wrong with my eyebrows—as eyebrows.'

Frowning, the Chief Librarian remarked: 'They are undoubtedly unusual.' He placed his hand so calmly and with such professional ease under my chin, veil and all, tilting my veiled face closer, that I submitted as to a physician, by closing my eyes. Critically he observed: 'These eyebrows are delicately winged and give your face a look less than human. But keep them so. Our ladies paint theirs too heavily. Be good enough to open your eyes for the eyebrows are slightly disturbing. They resemble too closely the antennae of a butterfly in relief.'

Astonished, I asked: 'What does that signify?'

'Acute sensibility which might deteriorate into perpetual restlessness.' With a warning shake of his head he added, 'Indeed, could those two eyebrows spring forward freely, you might next soar to Samarkand or, later, distract the Emperor of China.'

But I scarcely heard him now—I had suddenly taken a step back: 'Merciful heavens, I have just remembered a prophecy! How terrible all this is—another fortune-teller read my fate years ago. Forgive me, but my blood is running cold!' Moving backwards like a sleep-walker, I subsided abruptly on the white divan and stared at the Chief Librarian aghast. 'When I was a girl of twelve a Negress with second sight foretold that I would be taken prisoner at sea, brought to a vast palace where I would bear a son who would one day become a great King—and that at the height of my happiness—'

'Did you say happiness?'

'Yes, yes, that was the prophecy—but at its height my life would pass away like a dream.'

'An admirable end.'

I clasped my shoulders and rocked to and fro: 'That I could have forgotten that dreadful prophecy—when here I am fulfilling it. . . . Oh, don't you see that the petition is hopeless? I am doomed to remain here . . . *doomed.*'

Sternly, for the first time, the Chief Librarian addressed me: 'Reluctant Guest, your candour is excessive—indeed, less than gracious.'

'Oh, don't reproach me,' I cried mournfully. 'I am still a stranger—'

'And assuredly of more than an age to leave the parental roof!'

I ceased to rock. 'Ever since I arrived in Turkey I have been made to feel that I am Methuselah's mother!'

With a little bow he said: 'As you will not remove your veil, I am not in a position to condole or congratulate. But I can relate an anecdote, famous in the East, on the danger of tactlessness.'

Despite myself I brightened. 'Oh, do! I love a story. I can listen to Blanche by the hour.'

Now seated, the Chief Librarian folded his arms and said tersely: 'This story does not belong to Blanche.'

But by this time I had become accustomed to his staid manner. I nodded encouragingly and he continued:

'It belongs to the poet Nizami and concerns the Persian King Bahram who loved a Tartar female called Fitna, a harpist, who accompanied him on all his hunting expeditions. One day, Reluctant Guest, this tactless Fitna challenged the King to transfix the hind hoof of a wild ass to its ear with a single arrow. There are such women. Nevertheless, the King shot a pellet of clay and grazed the creature's ear—then, when it put up its hind hoof to scratch, the King shot his arrow and pinned both ear and hoof together. But all that the tactless Fitna said was: "Practice makes perfect." Such women are yet more numerous. Yet, understandably, this retort of Fitna's so incensed the King that he ordered her death at once. But, being a sentimentalist at heart, he departed before this took place. Fitna, who could be plausible enough with inferiors—and such women are legion—persuaded a courtier to spare her life and to conceal her in a deserted shooting lodge. Years passed, as years will. Then one day, in a distant city, the King himself witnessed an amazing sight—a veiled woman who daily carried a full-grown cow on her shoulders up sixty steps. With his habitual generosity the King declared this to be one of the marvels of the age. But when the woman was brought before him, with humbly bowed head, she admitted: "Sire, it is nothing. When the cow was a new-born calf I carried it thus, and ever since, though it grew daily heavier, I never failed to carry it upstairs. Practice makes perfect." With these memorable words, the King recognized his lost love and graciously permitted her to return to his harp—'

The Chief Librarian paused. 'But posterity has shuddered ever since for that unhappy instrument!'

I laughed outright. And as he had risen, I too rose and held out my hand. 'Oh, thank you—thank you—for a little I have forgotten my troubles.'

Retaining my hand, he said: 'This Guest-in-a-thousand only needs patience and a little more courage.'

'Yes, yes, I must show more courage. I must go on with the petition. I must remember that I am a Dubuc de Rivery.'

'That name is pronounced by its owner as if it were a spell to intoxicate.'

'And why not?' I asked merrily. 'It is an old name and an honourable one.' Hastily I added: 'As no doubt yours is too.'

'No doubt at all of that.' He appeared to have forgotten that he still held my hand, for absent-mindedly, with it still enclosed in his, he next crossed his arms upon his breast. Yet his manner remained so formal that I was at a loss how to recover my hand. 'Over five hundred years, in direct descent.'

Momentarily I forgot my hand. 'But that is fabulous. . . . How wonderful for you! Why, it must also land you in The Ark with Noah—on your own Mount Ararat!'

He bowed above his crossed arms, with something like a smile—'Where no doubt we first met.'

Laughing, I said: 'I think I can just remember!'

'You were,' he added, 'pining to escape there too.'

'Well, and no wonder!' I humoured him, 'so were you!'

'Never—beside you,' he said politely. 'Tell me, were you, or were you not, Noah's first Kadine?'

'No, no,' I reminded him, 'you've forgotten our *earlier* conversation. I was the dove that Noah released!'

'Ha!' he said with a touch of his earlier stiffness. 'But the dove returned to the Ark—be good enough to remember. A creature graced with gratitude.'

I was silent for a second. 'Like Blanche, you make me feel ashamed. I have *not* been grateful. The ship bound for Martinique sprang a leak—we should all have been drowned had that other ship not over-hauled us—'

More mildly he said: 'Come, we met long before that, and you know it. Think back before the Ark and the flood—to a celestial peace, where in the fields of light you were a star, encircled by the crescent moon.'

This image touched and pleased me. Smiling, I said: 'Ah, sir, the beauty of the crescent moon on the Turkish flag is that its arms are open—I was then free to come and go . . . to come and go!'

At these words he released my hand and, frowning, moved abruptly back to the lectern.

Nonplussed, I feared that I had offended him—that I had better disappear before making matters worse. His expression was now both gloomy and forbidding. But at the first archway I ran back to the lectern.

Somewhat breathlessly I said: 'Sir, I would not leave you anxious. If the petition fails, I shall not ask you to help me further.'

Still frowning, he demanded: 'And why not, may we ask?'

'You have been very pleasant—and, somehow . . .' I hesitated, bewildered by my own mixed feelings, 'I would not wish you to run any risk. Now that I know you better—I must not bring you danger.'

Scarcely glancing at him, I curtseyed as deeply as if he had been the Kisslar Agassi and then, turning, skimmed towards the archway.

Barely had I reached it when the Chief Librarian called out in that official voice of his:

'Stop! Repeat that fascinating exercise with these draperies.'

Laughing, I did so where I stood—happier to part on this pleasant note. 'Adieu, sir,' I replied, 'I'm sure you cannot be aware of it, but at times the Turkish manner is somewhat autocratic!'

And, in farewell, to soften this slight reproof, I waved him almost—but not quite—an airy kiss. . .

# 9. THE FOUNTAIN-COURT

FOR the next two days I was more than hopeful—I was oddly exhilarated, restless, eager. I wondered when the Kisslar Agassi would call, so that I might glean more information about the Chief Librarian and, of course, the progress of the petition.

But His Highess did not appear. And I had ample leisure in which to realize how unusual it was to have met two such remarkable men in that short time. I recognized that each was, in his different way, unique . . . and I fell to musing on the possibility of meeting other persons of interest in this place. It seemed to me now more than likely. The Seraglio was certainly utterly unlike anything I had imagined.

All at once I remembered Joséphine's remark that she and I would soon be returning to Martinique and a basket-chair on the balcony! Unbidden, the thought arose: if the worst comes to the worst here and I am not released because I am the gift of the Dey of Algiers, yet if the Sultan himself ignores me (and I knew now that this was more than likely), life in this place might have happiness too, and its own liveliness!

But no Joséphine, no Eugène, no little Hortense! It shocked me that I should have forgotten them and my bereft guardian even for a second.

Yet that meeting with the Chief Librarian continued to dominate. It flattered me to think that he had so quickly felt at home with me, despite his shy, stiff nature—as the absent-minded retention of my hand had proved. Then, too, from the start our conversation had flowed freely—I had actually been able to express annoyance once or twice, which is ever a relief! The whole encounter had been effortless. In his quiet way he was undoubtedly impressive. What he said carried weight. And now that I considered him in solitude (a solitude so like his own, poor man), I felt increasing admiration. Moreover, a curious attribute set him apart from any other person I had known—his personality was quite as vivid in absence! This was a feature I had not found in any other friend before—

Indeed, during the last two days once or twice I had had a sudden but silent intimation that he too dwelt on me in thought. This magnetic experience was so swift and so arresting each time that my heart invariably lost a beat—but I will not deny that the sensation was also pleasurable! Then I remembered the petition he was preparing—I reminded myself that would explain this curious, sightless contact . . .

I also recalled his various attachments—as he had called them—wondering now how serious these had been.

But not until the three petitions, with their French translations, arrived by messenger did I realize that the Chief Librarian was more than remarkable—he was noble. Even the third, and least urgent petition would have softened any heart.

Now that my case was phrased so generously, I awakened fully to the perfect courtesy which had made such a plea possible—to the grace of the hospitality on which I was turning my back.

This caused me a perplexing pang. I found myself marvelling afresh at the Chief Librarian's insight and compassion. I could only hope and pray that his known assistance would not endanger him with His Imperial Majesty. The Turkish script was quite beyond my skill to copy—and recollecting that warning of the Sultan's irritability on this subject, I decided to proffer the Chief Librarian's as my own. If only I might thank him here and now—

But our mediator, the Kisslar Agassi, had not yet appeared, and I knew that I must await his arrival before I could hope for another visit to the Nizami Library. Yet a new and tender happiness, inexplicable but wholly delightful, sustained me. Now that I held the petition (indeed, three), haste on the score of my departure no longer seemed imperative. An interval in which to recover from my earlier alarms seemed advisable—before I drew the Sultan's attention to myself.

And in a spirit of sweet content I sat outside that evening, for the first time, in the deserted fountain-court. Through the dim, warm air starlight was not yet visible; only the fountain was distinct, springing like a white ostrich feather in the gloom, among the shadows of shrubs and early summer flowers. High above the Seraglio walls, at present hung with wistaria, rose the Minaret which later would flash like a lighthouse in the dark. Blanche sat opposite in the scented stillness, fanning us both alternately.

Suddenly the voice of the Muezzin was heard from the tower calling the night-azan. There he stood in the Minaret, facing the direction of Mecca, in that immemorial attitude, with his two forefingers in his ears, uttering the call to prayer:

'Most High! There is no god but the one God! Mahomet is the Prophet of God. Come to prayer! Come to the Temple of Life.'

While this voice pierced the warm evening air Blanche ceased to use the fan, and she and I remained reverently silent for some time after it faded. Then I admitted:

'Blanche, the poetry of this place grows upon me like a spell. I remember also our Mother Superior's words: "Do not reject what is at hand to dream of something else." We must enjoy this meantime.'

'Mamzelle, that's the most common-sensible thing you've said since we landed!'

'And the three petitions sent me by the Chief Librarian today are *all* so moving that I am certain now that we are as good as gone! Hidden away, that man must have the heart of an angel. I almost wept as I read his wonderful words on my behalf.'

'As good as gone!' Blanche sat bolt upright. 'Mamzelle, I pray you're wrong. The thought of that sea voyage with no Dey of Algiers waiting for us this time turns me right over! Now, mark my words, no sooner are you back in Martinique than you'll be pining for this superior place. And no power on earth will get us here again.'

I stifled the quick retort that home ties came first—remembering just in time that Blanche had already sacrificed eight years of these to be with me at the Convent. Martinique and our familiar circle there must certainly have changed since we left it nearly a decade ago—Instead I reminded her of all that the Chief Librarian had done to aid us, of how grateful we should be. I could not deny myself the luxury of mentioning that remarkable man for (as I thought) perhaps the second or third time.

'Mamzelle,' she said impatiently, 'you've done nothing but talk of that gentleman since you saw him at that Library. And now if he's bent on getting rid of you, 'gainst all that His Highness has warned, it doesn't make sense to me. No, I don't trust that

Librarian and his petition further than I'd trust the Greek Interpreter—and that's flat!'

My indignant rejoinder was never uttered. At that instant, with startling suddenness, the tuck of a drum was heard at hand. And side by side with its uniformed drummer the Interpreter himself appeared at the fountain—to Blanche's dismay!

On this occasion he made the Turkish salutation with the utmost respect:

'Worshipful Lady, in Turkey the new day begins at sunset. This is *tomorrow*! Therefore, today, at two hours before the next sunset, our Sublime Sovereign, Emperor of the True Believers, Shadow of Allah upon Earth, He who is the glory of the House of Osman, summons his entire Court to the Audience Chamber. . .'

At this point the drummer gave another rataplan on the drum and the Interpreter continued:

'Gala attire will be worn. All ladies will arrive unveiled. His Highness the Kisslar Agassi desires me to state that on this notable occasion the gift from the Dey of Algiers will be presented with all suitable distinction: She who is to be known henceforth in the Seraglio as Naksh, which being interpreted is: A Picture of Beauty. His Highness the Kisslar Agassi graciously invites her to bring her petition should she so desire. . .'

Again the Interpreter gave the full Turkish salutation, and to a prolonged rataplan on the drum, both he and the drummer vanished in the direction of the main building.

For a minute I sat there stupefied.

For once my wish had come true too soon. To-morrow with its hopeful possibility was already here—and I could not, for the life of me, understand why this should now leave me hesitant . . . .

# 10. PRESENTATION OF THE PETITION

THE following afternoon was one of preparation. From the Interpreter Blanche had heard that Court robes on such an occasion were invariably superb. With some sense I decided on simplicity, as I could not hope to equal these imagined splendours. The oriental clothes already afforded me were enchanting, but scarcely magnificent. I would go in white—there was something mild and mollifying about white . . . in a word, persuasive. But Blanche was dead against white: 'Mamzelle, you're going to look as lively in that as a candle at a bonfire!'

And to my surprise, shortly before I dressed, other apparel arrived which almost took my breath away, so exquisite were both colour and quality: silver draperies over trousers and tunic the shade of a damask rose. This time the silver slippers fitted to perfection. A small Turkish boy in a tasselled fez bore a phial of perfume which, the Interpreter informed me, had been especially created for Naksh by the Court perfumier. Later, the aroma it dispelled proved to be that of white jasmine—cool, fresh, fragrant.

I dressed with delight. I had no longer any fear that I would be the victim of a predatory Sultan—indeed, I fully realized now that both ignorance and self-importance lay behind that dread. Yet increasingly it had been borne in upon me how rigid protocol was here. The danger of my continued imprisonment lay in the fact that I was a gift from the Dey of Algiers. . . . But had not the Kisslar Agassi assured me that His Imperial Majesty was as generous as he was all-powerful?

At that stage I was mercifully unaware that quite apart from these considerations, no woman ever leaves the Seraglio who has once entered it—that a courteous and infinite patience was simply paving my way to acceptance of this fact . . . as it did with any of the few reluctantly imprisoned there.

Confidently, therefore, I joined the escort awaiting me in the Atrium. At the same time I felt a perplexing pang each time I remembered the Chief Librarian and my possible departure. Would I catch a glimpse of him today at Court? Blanche had brushed my hair until it shone like a shower of light beneath the silver web flung back from my face on this occasion. Later, I rejoiced that I had worn no jewels. Amid that galaxy, so rich in ornament and design, my silver and rose attire remained that of a flower. In my hand I carried a parchment scroll—the petition.

The Audience Chamber which I now saw for the first time has dazzled potentates, kings, ambassadors—its effect on an ingenuous convent pupil may be imagined. The last to arrive on this particular occasion, I was almost stunned by the splendour of the assembly. I completely forgot to look around for a glimpse of the Chief Librarian. At first I could not distinguish detail—the dense pageant shimmered. Then, gradually, as I advanced with my escort in this ceremonial hush, the two majestic Veiled Thrones ahead imposed their own order on my confusion—

In the brief period of waiting that next ensued I realized that the Court had already taken up what were probably established positions. On my left in front, and a little apart, stood a dark, vibrant-looking woman with a pale rather listless boy—and although I did not know it then, I had my first unforgettable glimpse of the Persian Kadine and her son, Prince Mustapha.

Then, from the right hand of the centre Veiled Throne, His Highness the Kisslar Agassi came forward to meet me and took up his position beside me. In a low but kindly voice which I alone heard, he said:

'You have nothing to fear. But do not present the

petition until I give you a sign. This will depend on His Imperial Majesty's indications.'

'Thank you,' I whispered. 'I understand.'

'Gentle Lady, be careful in speech when you advance alone to the throne, for every word will be translated by the Interpreter in courtesy to the Court. Unless, of course, the Sultan orders the Court to withdraw—which is most unlikely.'

Trembling a little now, I answered: 'I will do my best.' Glancing up, I had barely time to see the Interpreter—standing at some little distance from the Veiled Throne—when a fanfare sounded. And as I had been warned, every woman present assumed the Court posture: with head thrown back and hands crossed on breast.

The towering gold curtains of the Throne were swept back by the courtiers on either side of it—belatedly I remembered posture, but instead of flinging my head back, confused, I bent it forward on my crossed hands, as if in prayer. Earlier that day the Interpreter had mentioned that through the second diaphanous curtain I might not catch more than a glimpse of the Sultan. Privately, this had been something of a relief to me. After all, a glimpse was all that Blanche had caught from the window, as even on his charger banners always partially concealed him.

With lowered head I waited, as the fanfare died away. Then I heard an incisive voice speak in

Turkish from behind the thin curtain— At once the Interpreter translated in French:

'Greetings, Balthazar . . . speak.'

The Kisslar Agassi addressed the throne in French:

'Sire, the Court tenders its utmost homage and perpetual devotion. As Kisslar Agassi, I beg to present to Your Imperial Majesty this gentle lady, a gift from the Dey of Algiers—known now in the Seraglio as Naksh . . . the Picture of Beauty.'

Swiftly and tonelessly the Interpreter repeated in Turkish: 'A gentle lady, a gift from the Dey of Algiers known now . . . as Naksh.'

The Sultan's voice came from behind the filmy curtain in somewhat harsh French.

'Naksh, you are welcome to Our Court, as the notable gift of the Dey of Algiers. We are now disposed to hear some news of Our friend the Dey. Balthazar, the Court may withdraw.'

Trembling with the realization that I had no news to give of the detestable Dey of Algiers—a wholly unforeseen predicament—I heard the Interpreter translate the Sultan's words far too swiftly. The Kisslar Agassi whispered to me: 'You will later kneel on that cushion before the Throne—'

Years later I learned that as the Court, accompanied by the Kisslar Agassi, withdrew, smiling glances were exchanged while soft music played the assembly out.

Rooted to the spot, I still dared not raise my eyes. Again the Sultan spoke, and such was my confusion that I did not know whether his voice or his French was discordant—I only knew I was afraid.

'Naksh, come forward.'

Still with bowed head, I advanced and knelt on the small cushion placed for me on one of the shallow steps to the Throne.

Then, from behind the curtain, the Sultan said quietly but distinctly: 'Reluctant Guest—look up!'

I raised my head and through that veil as thin as vapour saw him for the first time clearly. Horrified, I cried: 'You!'

Regardless of etiquette, I rose, gazing at the Chief Librarian speechless with shock and indignation. Indeed, nothing can better reveal my immaturity and the confidence which the Chief Librarian had earlier aroused than the fact that I now completely lost my head. 'I can't believe it,' I exclaimed. 'How terrible!'

'Impassioned One, the Chief Librarian asks your forgiveness. Here too as at the Convent we must sometimes call a spade a spade. With strangers preliminary precautions are essential.'

But I was between tears and fury, for to me he still remained the Chief Librarian: 'What a trick—to dupe me, to win my confidence!'

'Alas,' came the calm reply, 'unlike the Chief

Librarian, the Sultan must take care. Hence that little comedy in the Library.'

'*Comedy!*' I echoed stupidly, for now the full force of the situation hit me; the reserved, attentive librarian to whom I had almost lost my heart was now revealed as this subtle foreigner to whom I had exposed its hopes and fears. 'Oh, what a blow this is—I shall never forgive him,' I added wildly.

'Explosive Guest—to which personage do you refer?'

Stung by the word comedy and recovering now through wounded pride, I stepped backwards on to the gleaming floor and swept him a profound curtsey. 'Sire,' I said coldly, 'trifles like my unhappiness should concern myself alone.'

Pleasantly, reflectively, the Sultan said: 'The Chief Librarian knew nothing of the human heart, did he?'

I flared again. 'He did, he did—or so I thought from the petitions . . . and now the whole thing is illusion. I am without a friend.'

Blandly the Sultan replied. 'You have three petitions to fall back upon. We are curious to know which you have brought—' and he held out his hand for it.

But reacting in sudden fear, I clasped the petition to me. 'No, no—you cannot have it now.'

'Cannot?' he said icily, and there was that in his

tone that alarmed me far more than the Dey of Algiers had done.

Between an exclamation and a sob, I handed it over. He studied it for a second. Then he asked amicably:

'This was the third petition—the one least likely to succeed. Why did the Reluctant Guest bring this one?'

I drew myself up. As once with the Dey of Algiers, I was for the moment beyond fear. I stared at him, almost with hate, and when next I spoke it was quite calmly:

'Sire, Your Imperial Majesty most cleverly snared first my confidence, and now this confession. As I have nothing more to lose, I admit the truth which I have just recognized. But in giving it I am a changed person . . . I brought the third petition as I no longer wished so eagerly to return to Martinique. I thought I had found a friend here—a friend of integrity . . . someone on whom I could rely. Now I have lost not only my home—but all confidence. A much graver matter.'

'Graver indeed,' and he actually smiled. 'Yet your customary vitality is now—if anything—excessive. Reluctant Guest, the Chief Librarian's heart which you have obviously stolen has not been a good exchange. It has chilled you to the bone.'

'Sire, you are mistaken,' my answer came like a flash, 'if I almost lost my heart it was to a man who had no existence—he was not even a ghost. I shall never make such a mistake again.' Frigidly I added: 'I have only one wish left which I beg Your Imperial Majesty to grant.'

'Speak.'

'The privacy of my own room.'

Calmly he said: 'This northern soul of yours is fiercely unforgiving. Go in peace—and remain in it.'

'Sire, I thank you—' but as I rose from my curtsey he said sharply:

'Take off your slipper.'

Astonished, I stared at him, doubting my ears. 'My slipper?'

'Your slipper,' he repeated impatiently, and held out his hand for it.

Bemused, I still hesitated: 'What is the matter with it?' Apprehensively, I handed it to him, through the veil.

Briefly the Sultan said: 'You may go.'

But I hesitated again, glancing down at my bare foot. Puzzled, I spoke aloud—in my impulsive way. 'Now I shall have to hop all the way home—back, I mean.' And I proceeded to move backwards.

'Stop,' the Sultan said tonelessly. Without a sound he clapped his hands. At once the deaf-mute slave nearest the Throne stepped forward. The Sultan pointed to my one slipperless foot. The slave bowed, then blew on an ivory whistle—

The next minute two bearers with a small gilt

sedan-chair ran in from the far end of the Chamber and stopped beside me. Only then did I realize that this was an immediate answer to my need. Overcome now by this consideration which my confusion had exacted, I stepped into the little chair. Behind its tiny window I bowed to the Throne, blushing.

Impassively the Sultan said: 'Now the Traveller will not have to hop all the way to Martinique.'

Somewhat to my surprise, the sedan-chair still remained stationary. The bearers apparently awaited some signal—but by now the festivity of my departure was almost too much for me. I leaned from the tiny window—speaking with a gasp and my first smile:

'Sire, I thank you . . . it is a very beautiful chair.'

The Sultan did not reply. Instead, to my bewilderment, he placed the silver slipper which he held inside the green Order that crossed his breast—the Grand Cordon of the Osmanli.

Immobile now, he no longer seemed to see us—and at once the bearers ran out in a long curving line between the pillars . . . .

## 11. BRIEF NIGHTMARE

THAT night my head was in a whirl. The Sultan's last word had been Martinique. I was certain that my departure was now a matter of days, but I was careful to say nothing of this to Blanche. I felt I could stand no further argument just then. She would know soon enough.

Was that final perplexing request of the Sultan for my slipper a courteous Turkish compliment—a delicate attempt to save the guest's hurt pride—much as a Frenchman might ask for a flower or a glove? Already I knew the Oriental reverence accorded any guest. Was this the explanation? I did not know, and already Blanche was besieging me for news . . . .

As well as I could, I gave her an account of the Court assembly. In answer to her eager questions on the Sultan's appearance, I replied hastily that he had remained more or less veiled. A potentate, I added truthfully enough, who was still a mystery to me—and likely to continue so. . . . I admitted that he had received me graciously, and that he had retained the petition. Doubtless I should have an official answer later. Next she wished to know what had happened to my new slipper.

'Lost,' I told her.

'You lost your slipper the first time you go to Court? Mamzelle, you are not a baby. What can they think of us here? Such a beautiful shoe too.'

As she seemed to take its disappearance as a personal reflection, I retorted tartly:

'They have presented me with a sedan-chair and two bearers—an admirable exchange.'

She threw up her hands at that, and again declared that the entire Turkish nation derived from heaven. For once I found Blanche an enormous effort that evening. I longed to be alone, yet also dreaded the time when I should be confronted by my own thoughts.

And sure enough, alone in my bedchamber where recently my mind had dwelt so genially on my new friend, chagrin ebbed to reveal a dismal loss. The Chief Librarian, fellow-prisoner and companion in solitude, had gone forever. That redoubtable personality was not even a phantom—he was a hoax. Although in my youthful inexperience I did not know it then, I was suffering the sharp disillusion of first love dashed as the cup is raised. Immature for my age, my sense of humour was still intermittent! I only knew that the more I thought of that cynical Sultan who bore such a damaging resemblance to him, the more I detested him. 'A little comedy,' he had called that moving encounter in the library when I had entrusted him with my life—and possibly Blanche's also! Humiliation was complete, too, when I remembered how much the Sultan had now guessed of my earlier tender interest from the choice of the third petition. Truly I must have been bewitched in that Library. Surely no woman from the beginning of time had later so completely given herself away!

As I lay on my divan, mortification, distress, confusion mounted like a fever. The night was hot and airless and I tossed from side to side. When at last I lay exhausted—coolly, dispassionately the Sultan's words recurred to me: 'The Sultan must take precautions with strangers.' Stories revived in my mind of reluctant slaves like myself who had actually poisoned bygone Emperors—sometimes in the love embrace itself. Possibly His Imperial Majesty had some reason there! And as one dread can evoke others, another historical incident rose to the surface. I remembered that earlier sinister Sultan who, tiring of his harem, had ordered each lady to be tied up in a sack, weighted with lead, and flung into the Bosphorus. Certain French kings had been notorious and Henry VIII of England ruthless in the extreme, but assuredly there had been nothing in Europe as wholesale as that dispatch of a Seraglio!

Alone in the darkness I forgot that my departure was imminent—that the Sultan's last word had been Martinique; my sense of nightmare mounted. I only knew that my reckless confidence in the Chief Librarian could quite easily have cost my life and that of Blanche too. Everything hinged on the Chief Librarian's nature—no, on the Sultan's mood. And in the eerie agitation of that hot summer night, once more there seemed to be two distinct men. Was I awake . . . or was I dreaming?

By morning I was in a high fever, oblivious of a distraught Blanche awakened by my cries. In my delirium I seemed to run endlessly up and down a long narrow corridor with glass doors—but to my horror, each time I tried to open a door and escape, it changed to a mirror reflecting the Sultan or the Dey of Algiers . . . .

Later, during convalescence, I learned that Blanche had at once dispatched the Interpreter to His Highness, the Kisslar Agassi, and that within an hour a Greek physician was in attendance. Thanks to his skill, my illness though sharp was short. The result of all this was that Blanche, insensible to my purgatorial experiences, again described as angelic the kindness of known and unknown Turkish friends. The Greek physician had completely reconciled her to the entire Greek race—our Interpreter included. 'Ah, Mamzelle, that Interpreter is sound enough in a crisis—yes, I must admit it!' At the height of her anxiety it seemed he had presented her with an unsolicited box of snuff the like of which she had never known before. It had not only cleared her head, it had left her, she assured me, as cool as a cucumber and equal to all my ravings! Privately, I thought it probable that this heaven-sent snuff had been drugged—and in my present humourless state that Blanche might now be an addict.

Yet so thankful was I to be out of my nightmare that after a week I mended apace. And as soon as I was able to rise, we heard that my physician had ordered a change of residence—described by the Interpreter as 'a more amiable solitude containing no unpleasant memories—only happy hopes.'

Borne by bearers in my gilt chair through a labyrinth of corridors empty of all but their sentries, it reminded me of that earlier but shorter journey to the Nizami Library. But now I had Blanche in close and comforting attendance—and we eventually emerged into the daylight of a very different site.

Bathed in sunshine, here at last was a small but separate residence, white and airy, festooned by wistaria, and set in its own garden. As if to prove this fact, the bearers ran with me right around it before pausing at its latticed entrance. I had time to notice that the garden itself was set in a half-hoop of dwarf weeping willows, a formal thicket such as this country knows how to group around its tiled courts. The little dwelling had a tiny blue dome resting on a pierced marble gallery through which subdued sunlight fell on the fountain of its hall below. Just then the garden was fragrant with lilac in full bloom—and Japanese maples were breaking into their first rosy leaf. This, I decided in my ignorance, must be a half-way house where departing guests, Ambassadors or Consuls were probably lodged, for although it also stood high it was appreciably nearer the sea. I did not, however, suggest its temporary nature to Blanche, for she was exclamatory with delight that at last we had a home of our own!

But I felt my heart soften somewhat to the Sultan who had shown such consideration for the Greek physician's prescription. Or was His Highness, the Kisslar Agassi, solely responsible? I could not determine and was left pondering again (but more pleasantly) on His Imperial Majesty.

I had begged for privacy and his reply had been: 'Go in peace and remain in it—' Assuredly nothing could be more secluded than this small embowered residence, with the towers and minarets alone visible above the tree tops.

In giving me the sedan-chair he had also said: 'Now you will not have to hop all the way to Martinique.' Why had I been so fearful? It was only a matter of time before I left.

And when the Kisslar Agassi paid his next visit, he too seemed to regard my eventual departure as a question of time, for with his benevolent yet whimsical smile he said: 'But, Gentle Lady, you are scarcely fit to travel yet!' which was true enough. I assured him that I would be patient—that indeed this would be a pleasure in such a place, surrounded by such kindness.

'Tomorrow,' he promised, 'a number of books in your own language will reach you here—to beguile your convalescence. Until you are able to visit the library again.'

At once I stiffened. 'Your Highness,' I said, 'my happy experience there proved more than a disillusionment—it ended as a shock. You, with your sensitive perception, will know exactly what I mean when I tell you that the Chief Librarian and His Imperial Majesty will ever remain for me as poles apart.'

For a second I had a fleeting impression that His Highness was about to laugh—but no, with suitable concern he replied:

'Gentle Lady, I know both very well, and I can assure you that they are one and the same man.'

I shook my head, flushing as humiliation revived: 'I thought he was a solitary like myself—another kind of prisoner in that Library. I opened my heart to him . . . the absurdity of it all!'

The Kisslar Agassi remained silent for a second,

and I realized that he was now as far from laughter as myself. Then with a short sigh he said:

'Gentle Lady, there was no absurdity. His Imperial Majesty is the loneliest man in his kingdom.'

Abruptly he rose to go, leaving me for once somewhat abashed in his presence . . . oddly at a loss.

## 12. THE PAVILION OF NAKSH

WHEN my actual change of heart took place I do not know, but looking back I suspect that these words of mild reproof were the beginning of my new life there.

Although I did not realize it at the time, it was during the complete solitude of the pavilion of Naksh that, slowly and invisibly, the lost Librarian came to merge with the absent Sultan. At the end of three weeks' convalescence I felt a certain restlessness which yet had nothing to do with my return to Martinique. Indeed, I told myself that if reassuring news could be sent there of my safety, I would gladly spend the summer in this beautiful place! I resolved to ask His Highness the Kisslar Agassi when next I saw him if such a message might be arranged for Martinique....

Meantime it seemed to me that this restlessness was a natural desire for visitors. 'Blanche,' I said once more, 'you spoke of flowers and delicacies that came when I was ill. Strange that no one calls now?'

'Mamzelle, have you lost mother-memory as well

then? Only two, three weeks ago you told His Highness the Kisslar Agassi that you wanted privacy. And this is what you're getting!'

It was unanswerably true. And the longer I sat there alone, the more clearly did I see my past behaviour as that of a spoiled child—the more I marvelled at the courtesy with which it had repeatedly been met. Again I remembered the parting words of the Mother Superior: 'Do not reject what is at hand to dream of something else....'

Yet rejection had been the order of my self-willed days ever since arrival here—until now ... when possibly acceptance might prove too late. Any day news could reach me that arrangements had been made for my departure ...

Pondering afresh the Sultan's farewell words: 'Go in peace and remain in it,' I was struck by the fact that it was an envoy almost identical with Reverend Mother's when she had said: 'Go in peace, my child, and remain in peace.' And she had added kindly: 'You have the virtue of constancy—there you will not be tempted so often.'

Was it this same constancy that made it so difficult for me now to forget the Chief Librarian—the first man to awaken my imagination?

During these silent weeks I repeatedly rehearsed the Sultan's last request. He had distinctly said: 'Take off your slipper' ... and then he had placed it in his bosom. To me a most unusual gesture. Yet possibly a conventional courtesy here—for not one word or one sign since. Three whole weeks ago now . . . Perhaps he did not know that I had been ill? Perhaps all this kindness had since come from the Kisslar Agassi? It was a sobering reflection.

And on looking back, I realized afresh that the chief attraction of the Chief Librarian had been that magnetic communion we shared in absence . . . What a wonderful experience that had been! Only now was I as grateful for it as I should have been. There was nothing of that invisible but unique harmony today, and it proved no comfort to recognize that I myself had somehow broken the spell.

Such were my thoughts when the fourth week began towards sunset. Seated in the garden on a low marble sofa which curved beside an ornamental fish pond, I could hear persistently the gentle plashing of water, the rhythmic cooing of pigeons. The fish pond lay midway between the house and a small pavilion which stood on a slight eminence at the far end of the grounds, overlooking the sea. This pavilion with its open, marble arches resembled a Greek temple of the winds, but within there was another circular divan piled with cushions, and a Persian-tiled floor. Its pillars framed a wide sweep of sky and sea, and there privacy was absolute, but I felt an increasing desire to be nearer the house and its gateway where lilacs had now given pride of place to roses. Not a breath had stirred today. Yet the frail foliage of the weeping willows which surrounded the property on two sides seemed to float perpetually in the still air. Only I was lifeless in this paradise on earth—

Impatiently I sprang up and sounded a little bronze gong beside me. In a few minutes Blanche bustled into the garden, bearing my guitar.

'Has anyone come? Is there any letter?'

'No, Mamzelle—whom do you expect?'

'It doesn't matter . . . Are you certain that you have *not* left my slipper at the entrance?'

'Mamzelle,' she protested with all the vigour of repressed impatience, 'I'm worn out checking that your slipper is not outside! All you can do is to beat that gong or to feed those poor fish to distraction. What's the matter with you, Honey? Here you are in a choice new home, with a garden of your own, and you can't settle! Didn't His Highness, Kisslar Agassi, tell you to visit that Library you were so crazy about?'

Hurriedly I re-seated myself. 'The Nizami Library is not as interesting as it was. They keep changing the staff.'

'Well, Mamzelle, if you can't study, for the love of mercy sew—or sing! Only let me get back to work—' and she plumped the guitar on to a cushion.

But I insisted: 'I think it very odd that no one ever calls—no ladies, no courtiers, no one at all—'

Before Blanche could reply, there came an ominous sound of kettledrums, a rumbling like distant thunder, and I shivered:

'What can that muffled rolling be?—we hear it off and on almost daily now.'

Blanche herself had paused. 'It's those Janissaries, Mamzelle. When they don't fancy the next meal at the barracks, they beat their kettledrums. Yet they get the best of everything in Turkey, so I'm told. Too much corn fires any horse!'

'These muffled drums are the only ugly thing in Stamboul,' I said slowly. 'I've a feeling that there's more behind them than we know. I wonder what the problem is?'

Blanche held up a warning finger. 'It's stopped . . . And sooner this time! Seems someone's cut them short—Good business too!'

As we spoke, with the swiftness of sunset in the East, evening advanced, but now a cheerful little fanfare was heard at hand—and again I jumped to my feet:

'Quick, quick, Blanche—this may be news!'

Turning towards the house, she inquired: 'Are you at home?'

'To anyone—to everyone . . . Oh, Blanche, use your intelligence!'

As she disappeared, I quickly adjusted my fez, my white tunic and draperies, and a few minutes later the Kisslar Agassi was shown into the garden.

The speed with which I ran to greet him proved what old friends we now were. His small retinue remained at the front entrance while I welcomed His Highness to the marble sofa, bestowing cushions right and left upon him—and Blanche hurried to bring glasses of sherbet.

As we sat sipping this, he said: 'Gentle Lady, I have an immediate item of news that is less welcome to me than it might be!'

I felt my smile fade. 'The Sultan permits me to return to Martinique?'

'No, Gentle Lady—is that still your wish? I had hoped you were now happier here.'

To my own amazement his words were like a reprieve! Earnestly I assured him: 'Oh, I am happier—much happier. But the last word that His Imperial Majesty said to me was Martinique . . . and I thought . . . I thought—I have heard nothing since.'

'Gentle Lady, I can no longer conceal from you that I have never known anyone leave the Imperial Harem.'

'Thank you,' I replied somewhat breathlessly, 'thank you for this frankness. It is almost a relief to know at last exactly where I am! Uncertainty is sometimes the worst of a situation. I had hoped to hear before this.'

He smiled kindly. 'Our beloved Padishah has been heavily engaged on State affairs these past weeks, but he hoped that the greater privacy of this house and park would please you?'

'Oh, it does, it does indeed! I'm quite ashamed that I've not made better use of my time since last I saw Your Highness. Spring passing into summer with so much beauty here seems to have unsettled me—but tomorrow I shall start my study of the Turkish language.'

'Gentle Lady, all this is blessed news from you. I no longer feel uneasy about the item I have brought. The Persian Kadine, mother of Mustapha, the Sultan's only son, has expressed a wish to visit you this evening.'

Again I felt the smile fading from my face. 'His only son?'

The Kisslar Agassi nodded. 'His only son—a rather delicate boy, unfortunately. The Persian Kadine is a charming, gifted woman, but I cannot believe that you and she will ever find much in common. Your ideals are different. Yet as Kadine it is natural that she should wish to meet you. And I advise you to see her. But I would counsel you always to remain at a discreet arm's distance! In fact,' he leaned forward and spoke in a lower tone,'it is imperative that at no time do you visit her palace without first letting me make all the arrangements for this.'

Mystified, I answered: 'Your Highness, I realize how little I know of the Imperial and other etiquette here, and I assure you that I shall never take any such step without your help.'

He rose. 'Then all will be well, Gentle Lady. I have told the Persian Kadine to call within an hour, unless she hears to the contrary. Now I shall leave you—for it may be better if you meet without too much ceremony.'

I curtseyed: 'But please come soon again, Your Highness—when you can spare the time. Always you bring comfort and courage.'

After he had gone, I sat back on the marble sofa feeling oddly winded. A charming, gifted woman who had given him a son . . . I could not fathom for the life of me then why this news should so deplete me. Vigorously I told myself how thankful I should be to realize the total unimportance of my presence there—

I lifted my guitar and for a time sat strumming, to drown thought, for this strange and unexpected journey through my own soul pained me . . . .

Perhaps twenty minutes later Blanche came bustling back—plainly flustered:

'Mamzelle, are you still at home to anyone and everyone? A lady has arrived with more attendants than His Highness!'

Apprehensively, I arose. 'A lady?'

'Tinkling with bells like a baby's rattle! But this lady is no baby, Mamzelle, so take care . . . for as sure as I stand here there's only one madame living that could handle this one—and that's Mother Superior.'

Swiftly I said, 'Show her here at once, Blanche—with the greatest respect. Take these glasses. And bring fresh sherbet.'

As Blanche disappeared, I hurriedly re-arranged the cushions, removed the guitar, and then sat down breathlessly.

A few minutes later the Persian Kadine entered the garden with several attendants, who remained discreetly at the entrance as she advanced to meet me.

The garden was now dim with evening after-glow, and in the dusk she seemed to me the most beautiful woman I had ever seen. She wore ruby-coloured draperies and gracefully flirted a jewelled fan in the warm air. Each time she did so, there came a minute cascade of sound from her silver bells. Overcome by this vision, I rose at once and curtseyed.

With ease and charm the Persian Kadine approached, and with both hands outstretched she led me back to my own marble sofa.

'Ah, Naksh—if you but knew the difficulty I have had to see you!' and she laughed delightedly. 'Yet poor as my French is, I felt I might be better than nothing—to one so far from home.'

'Madame,' I exclaimed, surprised and pleased, 'your French is perfect. It is more than kind of you to come!'

Playfully she shook her fan. 'Now, now—curiosity had a good deal to do with my benevolence! The Kisslar Agassi has been guarding you like a state secret—or a high explosive—and I said to the other ladies: "Can she be as dangerous or as beautiful as all that?" And here I am, the advance guard of many unknown friends of yours! Ready to tell them that you are more beautiful than we feared!'

The humorous raillery of her attitude was completely disarming, and by the time that Blanche returned with the sherbet, the Persian Kadine and I were laughing merrily. After serving us, Blanche, to my annoyance, departed with a long look and pursed lips of which my fluent guest happily remained oblivious. In an effortless way, entirely due to her own poise, we continued to exchange pleasantries and as we finished our sherbet we might have been acquaintances of long standing. Soon she had me laughing outright, for with the observation of a born mimic she proceeded to touch off first one and then another Seraglio character for my benefit.

By the time the moon rose and silvered the scene, this ready raconteur seemed to me a second Scheherazade!

'Madame,' I said, 'this has been so pleasant—and may I ask you to thank the other ladies also for their thought of me. At first I felt very much a stranger, I confess.'

The Persian Kadine nodded. 'Homesick, of course! I suffered agonies at first, but I daren't breathe a word, for I had besought my father to arrange my entrance here from Persia.'

I was astounded. 'You arranged it—without . . . without seeing?'

'Well, of course. Higher than this a woman cannot go! From the age of twelve I plagued my parents to secure my arrival here.' Tolerantly she laughed. 'But I hadn't bargained for homesickness. Later, pride prevented any mention of this to Persia! And of course I recovered.'

Softly I said: 'And your son would be a solace.'

Briskly she replied: 'He is a satisfaction—children can never be a solace. Too much of an exaction!' and she smiled indulgently. 'Now, this garden is a solace—don't you agree?'

Fervently I said, 'Oh, I do—each day in it ends better than it began!'

'What it is to be young! This garden with its pretty pavilion—' and she looked around almost amused, 'is a tiny duplicate of the one I had on arrival. Yes, once I had recovered from my nostalgia, those were wonderful days! Too wonderful to last. Once my son was born—pouf! romance ended. The Sultan's passion waned—but how understandable.'

'Understandable?' I was shocked. 'How could it be?'

'Unlike other Caliphs, he has spent less time in the

Cage—*that* was his revered mother's plan . . . a lady with *most* unconventional ideas!'

'The Cage—what is that?'

'The Seraglio, of course! Women mean less than nothing to our unique Padishah. He is both athlete and scholar—a wholly exceptional being, brilliant as a diamond, *and* as impervious.'

During those last speeches of the Kadine and unseen by us both, a tall man dressed in white had entered the garden from the path behind the pavilion and, as we discovered later, had heard every word.

Oblivious, I exclaimed, and now almost in tears, 'How terrible for you—such an experience would almost have broken my heart. What a blessing you are so brave!'

'And lucky,' she said genially. 'Just think—I might have had no child, or—horror of horrors,' playfully she snapped her fan, 'a daughter! Yes, I can assure you, Naksh, a daughter is no solace here. In fact a daughter is a fatal mistake! I had *many* anxious months before Mustapha was born. But, Allah be praised, I have my son! And although women mean little to the Sultan and romance less—I think His Imperial Majesty has a certain regard for my judgement—'

'Let Us not define that too closely now!' said a voice behind us in the unmistakable French of Marseilles.

The Persian Kadine rose in dismay but I, overcome by the sound of his voice and this alarming confrontation, remained seated and buried my face in my hands.

'Sire,' she exclaimed, 'I did not dream—'

'Nor did We,' he said politely, 'but possibly Our hostess finds your revelations something of a nightmare. In France the customs differ.'

In a tense voice she replied: 'Sire, I am completely overcome—lest you misunderstand my playful gossip. I crave leave to withdraw.'

At once I pulled myself together. I rose and made the Sultan a belated curtsey. Calmly he addressed the Persian Kadine: 'We wish you good night.'

My voice trembling, I said hastily: 'Madame, I thank you again for the courtesy of your visit.'

Stiffly the Kadine made the Turkish salutation, then swiftly vanished towards the house, where Blanche awaited at the entrance.

So stunned was I by these events that for support I found myself clinging to the marble back of the sofa.

The Sultan deliberately walked round the fish pond and now stood facing me at a little distance. The full moon had blandly transformed night into the semblance of gentle daylight, and I saw that he was dressed exactly as he had been in the Nizami Library. Absurd as it may seem, nothing could have restored my confidence so quickly.

'Be seated, Reluctant Guest,' and it was himself again who spoke. Thankfully I obeyed. 'You see before you,' he continued mildly, 'one who is for the moment neither Sultan nor Chief Librarian, but We hope a sovereign specific!'

I looked up quickly and for the first time smiled. 'Antidote, Sire?'

He inclined his head with a gleam of amusement, but in the instructive fashion of the Chief Librarian pursued: 'From the Greek *antidoton*, a medicine given to counteract poison.' He paused. 'The Kisslar Agassi informed Us of your visitor. And We then said to Ourself: If We are not welcome now, We never will be.'

And he remained standing there, with such grace and humility that, forgetting myself, I rose and ran to him with outstretched hands:

'Say no more, Sire—you are indeed welcome to this beautiful garden which you have lent me.'

Gently he took my outstretched hands and folded both within his own across his breast, yet lightly made things easy for me.

'That scoundrelly Librarian!' he remarked. 'To be cutout by Ourself at Our pompous worst is too much for human endurance!'

I smiled reminiscently—we might have been back in the Nizami Library: 'He was such a handsome man—and then all *his* tender attachments had come to nothing! That gave me confidence—

for what am I to think of the lady who has just left us?'

Quietly he said: 'Less than nothing. What is hers can never belong to another, but so small is this regard now that no generous soul would grudge it. She has even scandalized the goldfish—see how they gape! Let us sit in the pavilion. It has a wider horizon....'

Hand in hand, as if it were the most natural thing on earth, we went up the shallow circular steps to the pavilion. Moonlight fell brightly through its pillars—and in the warm distance we could glimpse the summer sea . . . and to this hour I can still recapture the scent of crimson roses then.

'Reluctant Guest,' he said when we were seated, 'why are you silent now? In the Library you thought that we were fellow-prisoners of a sort . . . surely confidences might be exchanged again?'

Gaily I told him—for he could always rally me from shyness—'Sire, I am thinking of my lost slipper . . . wondering what its fate has been?'

'It is worn out by State councils,' he replied, 'and the urgent beating of this heart. But with Our silent Guest, We too must remain silent.'

'No, no, Sire,' and fervently I admitted it now, 'you have been silent too long. The past three weeks, since my illness, have been the longest in history! And the constant thunder of those muffled drums filled me with foreboding.'

'Ah,' he said dryly, 'Our Janissaries brewing trouble with their soup! But today certain mischief-makers were rooted out—somewhat to their own surprise. Now there will be peace for a season. Such bodyguards always detest the rest of the army. Rancour is their chronic ailment.'

Puzzled, I exclaimed: 'But, Sire, this is a strange problem here—when you have so much water at hand.'

'*Water?*' he repeated, frowning.

I pointed between the pillars, 'Seas, I should have said—at your very doors. Armies soon sing small with navies to enclose them!'

He stared at me for a second. 'Out of the mouths of babes and sucklings . . . Yet to increase our navy would at once arouse suspicion.'

'But, Sire,' I exclaimed, '*must* it be called a navy? Could not special fleets of merchantmen be built here with the help of French or other foreign architects and engineers?'

Again he stared at me in silence, then abruptly said: 'Reluctant Guest, you would be more worthily placed at Our State council—than your lost slipper next this heart! Now We will trust you to forget entirely this naval flight of fancy—until a later date.'

I hesitated . . . 'And shall I still be here then?'

Grimly he said: 'You will be here till death shall part us. Does that alarm you now?'

'No, Sire,' I answered steadfastly, 'if you can also

assure me that death itself will never part us. . . That is the enduring guarantee.'

'Reluctant Guest,' he expostulated, 'this is the wildest extravagance! You wish Us signed and sealed for Eternity as well as time? One other only has desired this in Our lifetime.'

Again I hesitated . . . anxiously I asked: 'Sire, was—was she very important?'

'She was my Mother,' he said shortly, and then unexpectedly he sighed. 'In vain did I refuse to commit myself beyond time. The Empress would insist with the ingenuity of your sex: But Eternity is that vast tomorrow which is perpetual Today.'

I laughed from sheer happiness: 'Yes, yes, indeed! The Empress knew, Sire. Our Reverend Mother taught us that the Hebrew verb to believe means also to be firm, or to be constant.'

Briefly he said: 'One must also leave something to Allah! But is it love—or simply another meeting which you wish to secure in this celestial Tomorrow?'

Soberly I replied: 'Sire, I know this now. I would rather meet you after death than know I was your best-beloved *here*—or there.'

'Is that then the all-important end—to meet again?'

'Yes . . . with me it would be everything—whether you loved me or not.'

The Sultan smiled as he pointed through the pillars to a solitary, radiant star. 'Heaven seems to be in league with you, for there is Arcturus—the Shrine of Meeting! And astronomers warn us that if it were blotted out, it would leave a greater gap than would our own sun.'

I leaned forward and gazed at it devoutly. 'Of course it would—the Shrine of Meeting.'

But as I moved, the Sultan caught sight of the gold heart which I always wore on a chain round my neck. His voice at once became formal—

'What is this gold heart which you wear so closely?'

Fondly I replied, 'It holds the image of my dearest and nearest—' my voice faltered for a second, 'whom now I may never see again.'

Stiffly he said: 'We did not know that a Convent maiden would be permitted to wear such a symbol.'

Oblivious then of his growing displeasure, I exclaimed: 'It holds them both—my cousin Joséphine and her little son Eugène.' Opening the locket, I handed it to the Sultan.

He held it in the shaft of moonlight and more amiably remarked: 'It is a pleasing female face—but an erratic one.'

'Sire,' I protested, 'she has the most loving nature.'

'Nevertheless, she is erratic. But the boy's head shows balance. He will stay his course. What of his father?'

'Comte de Beauharnais has proved a misfortune. He had broken *all* his vows.'

'To break one vow is dishonour—to break all suggests imbecility. Is the husband of Joséphine deranged?'

Uneasily I amplified: 'I should have said: All his *marriage* vows.'

'There should be none. That European custom is preposterous. There must be equitable provision for each child and the mother. Then only can a family live in peace. But a vow is of major importance. Death is preferable to any default there. Domestic matters should be legally secured, without recourse to that dire risk—a broken vow.'

Between a gasp and a laugh I exclaimed: 'Oh, dear me, if I'm not careful, Sire, I shall soon believe every word you say!'

With the glimmer of a smile he said: 'Practice makes perfect. We do not despair.'

'Sire,' I paused a moment, 'I have a favour to ask—but I still do not feel as much at home with you as with the Chief Librarian. . . .'

'That infernal fellow again—Speak!'

'Would . . . would it be possible for me—now or later—to see Joséphine and the children here?'

To my dismay the Sultan made a sudden gesture as if he swept both me and the question despairingly from his sight. Then he rose and took some steps from me, until he stood facing the fish pond again.

'Sire!' mistaking his abrupt gesture for anger, I

ran towards him—then stopped half-way. As he turned, he noticed this.

Ironically he said: 'In the Library, you ran all the way back—ah, well, that was to another man!' Then he added harshly: 'No, Naksh, our customs are as the laws of the Medes and Persians—unalterable. It is impossible for you now either to see or to communicate personally with your people again. Like your revered Mother Superior at the Convent, We must again call a spade a spade. Here all is sacrificed—' and his voice became increasingly acid, 'for the benefit of one whom the poet Nizami described as a dead body with the soul of a man—but not journeying with the caravan, not one of its company.'

'No, no,' and now I ran to him urgently, 'that is not true—you are alive today, as you will be in time's tomorrow. Remember Arcturus, remember the Shrine of Meeting!'

But he no longer met me half-way. Rigidly he regarded me: 'Ah . . . We omitted to relate that in Syria Arcturus is known as the funeral bier—because of its slow and stately motion round the Pole. And Heraclitos, five hundred years before the Prophet Jesus, declared that Arcturus marks the boundary between East and West. It is no Shrine of Meeting, Naksh, but a frontier that divides.'

Beyond fear now, and in a greater dread, I

clasped my hands: 'I only know it as the Shrine of Meeting—as true of tomorrow as of today.'

Aloofly, with both hands on my shoulders, he replied with the utmost gravity: 'Today is the acid test, Unsuspecting Guest—year after year, without your own people! Possibly an extremity of loneliness, for We confess We would find it easier to absent Ourself than watch joy die within you. Yet what is the alternative for you? This life of the East, with customs alien to you? Shared with a stranger—of whom you are more than half afraid.'

'No, no,' almost in tears now I assured him. 'Never absent yourself. That day in the Library was the most unusual—yet the happiest of my life. I shall welcome the future here. I realize the difficulties with Joséphine. I promise not to ask again.'

Bitterly he said: 'Think what it has meant to Us to refuse this request! We, whose delight it would be to give you paradise on earth. But rest assured that news of your safety will be sent to Joséphine and to your guardian. News of *them* will always reach you through Our emissaries—although direct communication must remain impossible for you. Yet by this means you may still aid both Joséphine and her children continuously. Is this some small solace for life with a stranger?'

Sweetly I said: 'He himself is my solace. And, Sire, if I can accept today with joy and faith—surely you can believe in that other tomorrow?'

Amused, he shook his head. 'On this little matter of Eternity, you are as obdurate as the Empress!' but he folded me in his arms as he spoke. 'Shall We say that as this miracle of meeting has happened once, it is less unlikely to happen twice? Will that suffice?'

Smiling up at him, I answered: 'It is a bright start—and . . . and practice makes perfect!'

At this he gave his first full-throated laugh and swung me round until we faced the pavilion once more, two white-clad figures in the summer night. As we mounted the shallow steps, the star gleamed again between the pillars—

'All hail, Arcturus,' he cried, 'deal memorably with Us! Our pilgrimage has indeed begun. . . .'

# 13. THE BRITISH EMBASSY

THE next months brought happiness which I then believed could never be surpassed—and sometimes I was momentarily afraid that this unique experience was perhaps too good to last. Such foolishness, such lack of faith . . . for the further future was to hold a serenity and security immeasurably more valuable, as I grew to understand the Sultan better.

Before that first summer ended the Kisslar Agassi urged another domicile, but nothing would induce me to leave the pavilion. Childishly I associated my present joy with it—superstitiously I clung to it. Blanche also felt that it could not be bettered—and both of us continued there care-free. Our domestic problems were almost non-existent, for in the Seraglio all meals were cooked at central kitchens and then conveyed at speed on trays by bearers. To me it was a miracle that this delicious food remained hot—but it invariably did, and later courses could always be kept warm on our charcoal stove. Thus the first halcyon year drew to its close—and I remained thankfully in my pavilion.

But in Turkey tradition has a way of having the last word, and by next summer events occurred in the Seraglio which I was powerless to influence. These events had a far-reaching effect on Stamboul itself and on its foreign embassies as well—at one of which, on a certain night in July, a young British attaché had arrived who was, eventually, to become one of Turkey's staunchest friends.

This, then, is the account of his arrival on that crucial night of July 20th, 1785, a description which he gave us personally twenty-five years later . . . .

Vividly he evoked his first interview with the British Ambassador earlier that evening, at the Chancery office with its three wide arched windows framing the domes and turrets of Stamboul and, on this occasion, a great expanse of thunderous summer sky. There were, he told us, two shabby armchairs and a small coffee table set below the third window, but during this first interview the Ambassador's large writing-table dominated the scene, with two upright chairs vis-à-vis. The young attaché had a glimpse of a further business table to his right, the usual Foreign Office lists, the wire correspondence baskets, the punches, the little green silk tags. Anything less like the beauty and luxury of the Selamlik, he assured us, could not be imagined! But I, with a touch of European nostalgia, could readily picture that interior, with its faded map covering another wall, and on the shelf beside it the row of tobacco tins. In the corner, he remembered, there was a third derelict waste-paper basket which contained a walking-stick with a smart sun helmet balanced upon it . . . .

The middle-aged Ambassador on this occasion looked older than he was, the youthful attaché younger, for both were feeling the heat. The Ambassador periodically and efficiently wiped his brow, aloofly replacing his handkerchief each time. The attaché dabbed his face furtively and rarely, and for the rest chafed his handkerchief incessantly between hands which he hoped were hidden by the writing-table. During these feverish manœuvres his chief looked everywhere but at his subordinate, although the measured precision of his voice conveyed nothing of his irritation:

'You are certainly younger than I expected, but no doubt the daily round here will remedy that—Ha!'

'It's certainly rather warm, sir.'

'Thunder brewing—quite usual in July. To return to the point: the Councillor's illness means we are short-handed. I must brief you accordingly—in case of eventualities. Be good enough to note the following details—irrelevant though some may seem. In this legendary land,' his smile was perfunctory, 'nothing is irrelevant. The very mosquitoes mean business from birth.'

'Quite, sir!' With a gasp the unfortunate young

man added: 'As it's my first day here, I walked through the bazaar—I realize now this was a mistake. So I hope you'll excuse me—this interruption, I mean. I'm extremely sorry, sir, but . . . but—'

The Ambassador's eye flashed to his subordinate's face and his tone was now mild. 'What the devil's the matter with you?'

'If it's possible, sir—might I have a drink of water?'

'It's on the table—at your elbow.'

The attaché stared in despair. 'Sir, it's idiotic of me—but I can't see it.'

Silently the Ambassador rose and, leaning across the writing-table, took the stopper from a terracotta vase beside the young man.

'Good lord,' the latter exclaimed, 'I thought that was an ornament!' Then in further confusion he mopped his brow, 'Sir, is there by any chance a tumbler?'

'There is none. You drink it from the beaker.'

'Thank you, sir,' and he was about to gulp greedily—'But what about you? I mean to say—here am I drinking out of this?'

Impassively the Ambassador flicked his quill towards a duplicate terracotta vase at his own right hand. 'To resume: forget all you have heard of Turkey as the Sick Man of Europe and the East. For generations this absurd view has been current. But this Empire has succeeded longer than most in controlling and containing the corruption that afflicts all such. Its strength is founded on the character of the Turkish people. Consider the British Government's problem if it had to legislate for nine Irelands instead of one! The Turk has a genius for equality, and remember that it has always been the Imperial policy to sacrifice *no* section of its subject races for the betterment of any other race. Anomalies exist, but do not let these deceive you. For instance, the Janissaries represent the élite corps here. They are often in a state of ferment. For decades they have been pampered, their kettledrums an ominous warning of further exactions. Our agents report a growing jealousy among them of their own ally, Bulgaria! We must watch this situation. Above all, any indications from the Imperial Harem should be studied—few and far between as these may be.'

The young attaché was astonished: 'The Harem, sir?'

'The Harem,' the Ambassador repeated sharply. 'Women can hold remarkable power at the Imperial Court, hidden though they remain. The boy, Prince Mustapha, is the Sultan's only son. His Persian mother has the reputation of being an intriguer. She is known as the Persian Cat—and the boy is already dubbed the Cat's-Paw. Fortunately her intrigues are confined to the Ottoman Empire! So far she has shown no interest in Europe or the embassies here. Her uncles and cousins are high-ranking Janissary officers. But—and now I come to our present anxiety—for nearly a year the only woman in whom the Sultan has shown any interest is of French nationality, so rumour states. Should this woman chance to be educated, intelligent—we might expect events there to favour France. That would be a serious matter, but luckily few of these odalisques are educated. But should her child—whose birth is almost due—prove to be a son, *we must not forget that he will stand second for the throne.* The mother will at once be dowered with a palace, and considerable domestic influence. And the Porte itself will be warned of this major event by a salvo of artillery five times a day for seven days! In which case the British Embassy might then find itself playing second fiddle to the French Legation. By the way, I hope your French is adequate?'

Nervously the young attaché said: 'I hope so, sir. My Turkish is certainly better.'

The Ambassador was astonished, 'You speak Turkish well?'

'Yes, sir, from childhood. My father spent twenty years here, and translated much of their poetry. I found the language easy as a boy—that is to say: expressive. It is soft, like Latin, but copious, unlike Latin.'

Almost in consternation the Ambassador surveyed him. 'This is highly unusual for an Englishman—but none the less welcome, ha! To resume: Let us not forget that Mustapha is known to be a sickly boy. But of course the child whose birth is almost due may prove to be a daughter. *In which case there will be no salvoes!* The French mother's influence will then be lessened at Court. And the British Embassy will certainly shed no tears over that!'

Eagerly the young attaché exclaimed: 'Sir, my kavass drew my attention to unusual animation in the bazaar this evening—he had no idea that I spoke Turkish, of course. What I overheard was probably only superstitious gossip—' apologetically he hesitated.

The Ambassador frowned. 'Nothing is irrelevant in Stamboul. What did you hear?'

More diffidently the attaché said: 'That this child—should it prove to be a son—would fulfil an ancient prophecy. He would become one of the celebrated Emperors of all time. They actually gave him a name, sir! Mahmoud the Great.'

'Well, let us hope that the child proves to be a daughter! Should the French influence prevail, the effect on Europe could be serious. At once our importance here would be diminished. It might mean farewell eventually!'

As he spoke, with the convulsive thud of an unexpected physical force a salvo of artillery boomed through the sultry summer silence. The young attaché started violently, but the Ambassador held up his hand in warning . . .

Again and yet again the sound reverberated through Stamboul . . . Before the final detonation, the cheers of the populace in the street below the Embassy, the sound of racing feet swelled jubilantly. Like a wind through the oppressive night people were rushing joyfully from their homes . . . .

As the two Englishmen silently turned their faces to the thunderous July sky, the Ambassador said grimly:

'This may alter the map of Europe.'

## 14. FAMILY AUDIENCE

BEFORE I could be induced to leave my pavilion the Kisslar Agassi was obliged to make some startling revelations on the need for security measures. Tactfully but emphatically he stated that the baby and I were now liable to any of those dangers which threaten royalty everywhere. At first I found this difficult to credit, surrounded as we both were by such obvious enthusiasm and kindness, but I had to comply at once. And a year was to pass before I realized that on the birth of Mahmoud the Court had, overnight, divided into a Persian and a French party. In fact, the older Mahmoud grew, the larger also grew the French party!

During those early months in my palace, I discovered that I could go nowhere without a retinue—so, at that period, nowhere I went! The palace with its own bodyguard, its rigid rules and regulations completely disconcerted me. It took time for me to realize that the Kisslar Agassi had carefully chosen the household personnel, and that all were adroitly ready to guide me at each step. At first I might be said to have taken refuge in the nursery quarters! And in the nursery itself I also felt something of an exile for there Blanche reigned supreme—aided and abetted by the baby who, from start to finish there, showed a marked preference for her. Impossible to conceal from myself, or anyone else, that the infant's interest in me was strictly utilitarian—Blanche remained the love of his life. Yet apart from this chastening fact, he was a daily delight—a burly little baby whose health throughout never gave us the slightest anxiety. As he grew older Blanche never ceased to boast that he was a positive pleasure to rear, compared with his mother who, it now transpired, had been a fussy, finicky creature from her cradle. A very inexperienced mother still, I too was suitably impressed by the sunny stability of the baby. Week in, week out, he proved as amiable as he was alert.

'This child is a saint,' the infatuated Blanche insisted.

But the Sultan, holding him high in his arms when Mahmoud was two months old, triumphantly declared that he already bore a striking resemblance to one of his most alarming forebears—at which the baby, to our astonishment, laughed in his face, laughed with such gusto that, to our dismay, mirth passed into a paroxysm.

Angrily Blanche snatched him from us: 'A child should not be excited—he has almost killed himself trying to please you . . . There, there!' she reassured the baby. And back in her arms he quickly calmed—his face, becoming normal in colour, assumed its usual seraphic expression, and he continued to gaze at Blanche as if in sight of heaven.

'The rogue's a diplomat as well,' the Sultan murmured, for we were both a trifle jealous of Mahmoud's preference for Blanche. The apple of our eye seemed to know that he was the very light of Blanche's . . . .

At last I ventured on the first of several journeys by myself through my new home—an ancient building with a complexity of corridors and offices, its empty audience chambers austere with marble and alabaster. Even its galleried living rooms, hung with fabulous carpets, overpowered me, although the glowing Persian tiles appealed at sight, and there was a fascination in the overhanging windows screened by pierced woodwork—above all, in the fountain-courts revealed by each wide entrance. But to my then unaccustomed eye, this lofty wooden structure, with its marble and mosaic linings, its gilded bronze recesses, remained accessible yet aloof as some shadowed mosque. Over all, there was the faint musty smell of an old museum. And that first summer as I pattered through its silent vestibules, my solace was the scent of hayfields which drifted through the unglazed windows, and the chequered sunlight on the ancient tiles. Yet later, as my own happiness took root there, I ceased to find its atmosphere of antiquity oppressive. With time I was to become passionately fond of the palace. That it had also been the home of the Sultan's mother before she moved to the final seclusion of the Empress's domain also endeared it to me. Part of the wonder of my new life lay in the fact that I had, invisibly, known and loved her before I loved her son....

And now, upstairs was my own son—but the annals of one happy nursery are very like another! They pass with seasonal alternations—spring, summer, autumn, winter, year after year uniting to yield a harvest of robust but homely events which later enshrine themselves in the bland light of memory. Their burdens, as a rule, are the bearable ones imposed by heaven before the advent of those inflicted by mankind. And through all Mahmoud's boyish scrapes and adolescent errors, Blanche persisted in extolling the vision, the courage, which he was later to make his own. 'A being from a better world,' she would fondly insist—a description which I used to think fitted my gentle daughter Esmé more closely! But Blanche's approval of Esmé remained patronizing: 'Madame, that poor child is her mother all over again—without her mother's dash.' 'Dash?' I protested. 'Style, then, if it must be compliments today.'

The first friend I made at the palace was to

remain a life-long one. In my early and solitary expeditions there, I had a curious experience. As I peeped through a screen, I saw a wizened little gentleman with a thin clever face seated by himself in a small ante-room before a low table. He was unconscious of my scrutiny and his function puzzled me. Yet he appeared to be a person of some importance, for I noticed that he always had his meals before I did. Each time I peeped through the screen, there he was, eating away, with his head on one side which gave him a slightly sceptical expression. Later I learned that he was my taster—there to detect poison. I was as horrified on his account as on my own—and at once made his acquaintance. Alone, I walked round his screen but, happily, I now spoke Turkish fairly fluently. 'I shall never forgive myself,' I told him, 'if anything happens to you.' With a twinkle he assured me that he was less likely to be poisoned than any other man in Stamboul. He had the complete composure, the perfect courtesy that now seemed to me so characteristic of the Turk. My visit must have startled him, yet after some conversation I felt that he too had recognized that we were indeed old friends. His last words to me that first day I have never forgotten, nor his dry little smile: 'Revered Madame, neither you nor I will ever be poisoned, although we shall live to meet an identical death. The best of all—we shall both expire on a prayer.' There was that in him which convinced me then that this was the truth—and that he knew it. Some months later I asked him if he had any wish that I might gratify. After a certain hesitation he admitted a deep-seated desire to visit the Nizami Library. The Sultan, who had heard of my interest in Iskelib, did not at first consent. 'You have the most unsuitable predilection for persons connected with that place!' But shortly my friend was granted access on certain dates, and there he eventually met the Sultan himself, who later admitted to me that Iskelib's erudition was remarkable.

Slowly but surely I awoke to find myself at home there. Yet certain restrictions always seemed to me severe. Wine, so natural to France, was forbidden—as in every Moslem household. In fact, one of the first rumours to be circulated against me by the Persian party was that Mahmoud had been weaned on champagne, which accounted for his bogus vitality! I also found the fast of Ramadan a sore trial when, for one month each year, the households of the faithful must neither eat nor drink from dawn till sunset. But my children, earlier inured to this discipline, took it ultimately in their stride. Yet my Mother Superior of Nantes need not have feared indolence in her pupil. The Sultan believed in work as firmly as he did in probity—so there I strove to shine as well! In this lively, energetic atmosphere the children came to value leisure to the full.

As they grew older, leaving me more time, I

discovered in myself—and with increasing pleasure—a certain grasp of some of the problems presented by the country's administration. Frequently the Sultan and the Kisslar Agassi—sometimes separately, sometimes together—would sound me on my views as to this or that. And they never failed to consult me privately on any French issue that arose. How often then did I wish that I had made better use of my time at the Convent! Zealously now I studied any European newspapers and books that could be got. In fact, after a decade I had possibly a better understanding of certain questions than many people actively involved in the outer world.

Yet, as I was later to discover, both the Sultan and the Kisslar Agassi invariably concealed major difficulties concerning either the Selamlik or the Seraglio from me. I knew well enough, of course, as Mahmoud grew to handsome, resolute manhood, that envy, malice, resentment would take their toll, as in every life, for these evils are no less real at Court because more cunningly concealed. For years distrust of the French party poisoned the Persian coterie, and in return the French partisans intrigued with embarrassing success! But the Kisslar Agassi had a notable way of foiling both factions to their mutual confusion. He was the most able, as well as the most noble statesman I was ever to know. And so, despite the conflicting influences of French and Persian parties, my confidence grew in all I saw so equitably surmounting rancour. From constant contact with two unique men that impulsive and apprehensive Convent pupil steadily gained in faith and serenity.

Thus twenty-three years that were astonishingly tranquil passed for me . . . years having more than the enchantment of distance now, years which in retrospect reveal the lustre of a reality defeating both time and tragedy . . . .

# 15. INTERNATIONAL AUDIENCE

ONE week after Mahmoud's twenty-third birthday, crisis struck. The two royal parties were summoned to a private conclave in the Audience Chamber, and at the unusual hour of eight that summer morning.

As we awaited the advent of the Sultan in silence, the Persian family stood facing the Throne on the right-hand side; Mahmoud and I were as usual on the left. Before the Throne, at present veiled, and immediately in front of it there was a space, and a cushion on the steps to the Throne denoting some unknown arrival.

I had not seen the Sultan for two days but Mahmoud had spent the previous evening with him and it seemed odd to me that Mahmoud had not mentioned the reason for this meeting, at which no other members of the Court were present. The Throne attendants alone were here, and the Nubian slaves, of course, in the background, each stalwart against his pillar.

During this brief pause I glanced across at the Persian Kadine, anxious to smile to her—but she and

Mustapha would not catch my eye. As always, they preferred to remain distant . . . and suddenly I felt a swift impatience—a conviction that it was hopeless to go on wooing them like this. Unveiled as she and I were for audience, I realized afresh how much harder she had grown in appearance recently. None knew better than I that on social occasions her mocking little laugh which once had had a cuckoo-charm now scoffed openly at everyone, that her attitude to me nowadays was a studied courtesy which almost verged on insolence. Mustapha, in her energetic shadow, had become a pale thin man whose high shoulders suggested a perpetual shrug. Invariably he held his elbows as if for support. His glance was evasive, his manner withdrawn, but his speech had surprising precision. He was an able man, and if he had only contrived to like us better I might have found him lovable, for he too was the Sultan's son . . . Mahmoud was a complete contrast, with the easy charm of youth and health. At that time he radiated energy and an infectious merriment. Strangely enough, I sometimes had the feeling that the Persian Kadine was drawn to him despite herself. Mahmoud did not look as tall as his impressive father for he was of heavier build, and only in repose was the sturdy rectitude of his brow and bearing noticeable. Yet I was very proud of him!

Quickly I looked up at him now, to comfort

myself—I scarcely knew why. Imperceptibly he nodded, smiling....

A moment later we knew that the Sultan had arrived—and the curtains were withdrawn. At once the Kisslar Agassi, somewhat aged these days but regal as ever in his high hat and rich robe, stepped forward with his silver wand of office.

'Sire, Prince Mustapha and his mother desire to present to Your Imperial Majesty a cousin of the Persian Kadine's recently returned from Europe by way of France and Germany—the noted merchant Ali Mirza Effendi. He brings first-hand news from three capitals.'

'He is welcome,' the Sultan said in his impassive way.

At that, Ali Mirza moved from the Kisslar Agassi's side and stood in the empty space before the Throne. He was an elderly dignified man who at once gave an impression of reserve and probity. He made his salutation with the devoutness of a Mussulman, and then stood with the ease of a man of the world.

Graciously the Sultan addressed him: 'Your jewels continue to enrich Us. And We know you to be equally astute in your judgement of men and affairs. Your news, therefore, will be as valuable to Us.'

The merchant bowed, 'Sire, I wish my news were as welcome as it is valuable. But so distressing have I felt it that I urged Prince Mustapha to let me make it privately.'

Calmly the Sultan said: 'This audience could scarcely be more private.'

Ali Mirza made a deep bow to the Sultan and then, to my surprise, another to me on his right: 'Sire, I am well aware how highly Prince Mahmoud and his mother esteem the Empress Joséphine, and how painful my news of the Emperor Napoleon must be to them. I still hesitate to speak.'

The Sultan, glancing reflectively at the back of his own hand, replied: 'Doubtless Prince Mustapha and his mother had sound reason for their decision.'

'Sire, indeed we had!' and the Persian Kadine gave her bitter little laugh. 'To have imparted bad news of the Emperor of the French and his Consort in secret to your Imperial Majesty would have left us suspect. For this reason we desired that Prince Mahmoud and his mother be present.'

'And here they are,' the Sultan said. 'Speak.'

Earnestly I exclaimed: 'Sire, Prince Mustapha and his mother have been both wise and brave to do this. May I assure Ali Mirza Effendi that I remember with horror Napoleon Bonaparte's treacherous attack on Egypt. The fact that the Empress is my cousin made this harder still to forgive—' impulsively I turned in pleading to the Persian Kadine, 'Madame, you must believe this!'

She made me a cynical little bow—then respectfully addressed the Sultan: 'Sire, it will be remembered that the Egyptian *coup*, that whole perfidious campaign, was planned by Bonaparte while our Ambassador was fêted by him and the Directory. All Paris, we heard, took on the aspect of an Oriental pageant in compliment to Your Imperial Majesty. This, while the French schemed to possess the territory of your Moslem subjects. But then—' elaborately she shrugged, 'the French are, after all, the people who earlier celebrated their own revolution by placing a prostitute on the high altar of Notre Dame!'

Dispassionately the Sultan said: 'A callow intelligentsia, intoxicated by elementary excitements—waste no energy on such. Bonaparte got the drubbing he deserved in Egypt.'

Mustapha, unclasping his elbows, made an impatient sign to his mother for silence: 'Sire, the ladies are moving back in search of trouble. Unhappily the present offers more, as Ali Mirza can vouch. Despite Your Sublime Tolerance during these past ten years when this city has been blatantly invaded by French merchants, teachers, architects, engineers and what not, Napoleon Bonaparte by perfidy and war has brought Europe to chaos—finally crowning himself Emperor! With incredible generosity Your Imperial Majesty has turned a blind eye on the antics of this mountebank—but now Ali Mirza has discovered that the Ottoman Empire itself has been betrayed by this madman—our supposed ally!'

There was a moment's silence, then the Sultan addressed the merchant: 'Speak.'

Again the Persian bowed. 'Sire, on my recent travels I visited at Memel an elderly Persian lady who was for years the love of a Russian nobleman there. This man, before his death, spent a fortune on my jewels for her, and she is still *persona grata* with the Russian Court. The lady is a devout Moslem with whom I have kept in touch for thirty years. I would answer for her veracity with my own. On this last visit she informed me privately—and with horror—that on the seventh of last July Napoleon had concluded a secret treaty at Tilsit with our enemy the Czar of Russia. This treaty—' and he paused impressively, 'provides for the dismemberment of Turkey between them. For himself Napoleon has reserved Constantinople and has insisted on the evacuation by Russia of the Danubian provinces—*to allay the suspicions of the Sultan!* That is the core of their contract.' The Persian then added with dignity: 'In dismay and loathing, I am obliged to report this infamous bargain, of which nothing is yet known publicly.'

The Sultan inclined his head slightly. 'We thank you. It is not the first time you have brought Us notable information. Your report will be fully studied—your services long remembered.' He extended his hand and the Persian knelt to bow over it. Then, as he stepped back, the Sultan added briskly: 'Come, let Us see how the two Princes would handle this problem. What does Mustapha recommend?'

'Sire, an international revelation of the facts as swiftly as possible. Napoleon will then be arrested headlong on his course, as consternation among both allies and enemies will be widespread.'

'What does Mahmoud suggest?'

Alas, Mahmoud at once revealed the energy, the freedom of expression that belong to the French side of his nature. Later, he too was to prove inscrutable as occasion demanded, but with this difference: that it was then of set purpose and not of second nature as in the Sultan's case. Now he stepped forward with a laugh on his lips and dancing danger in his eyes:

'Sire, Mustapha's plan is much too generous for the Russian fox and the French vulture. Mine would be very different. I would reveal nothing of our discovery. Play possum. Outwit them at their own game until the moment that our trap is ready to spring—and then,' unexpectedly he did a double stamp with left, then right, foot. 'But first let us match duplicity with cunning!'

Shocked, I involuntarily exclaimed: 'Oh, no, Sire—I pray that this great Empire will never sink so low. Mustapha's way has strength and honour. Mahmoud's plan amazes and dismays me. I can scarcely believe my ears!'

The Sultan gave me a brief bow. 'Our own ears are more credulous. The views of both Princes will be considered later. Has the mother of Mustapha any observation to make?'

'Sire, the Empress Joséphine is the cousin of the mother of Mahmoud. The consternation she has just revealed expresses also her anxiety on Napoleon's behalf—' I started back on a moan of protest but she continued smoothly, 'This may be natural, Sire, but it is also dangerous. As the present catastrophe is a crisis that concerns the Ottoman Empire itself, I can only offer now my humble silence.'

The Sultan gave her also a brief polite bow. 'Your silence has spoken.' Without glancing at me, for indeed I was palpitating to reply, he raised his left hand, nearest me, in a slight but emphatic gesture of arrest. Once again I knew that I had failed—he would never make an oriental of me. I was no match for her—she was a brilliant diplomat. Yet only last week he had privately tried to comfort me: *But this We know: you could keep silence under duress—she could not.* A tribute I now felt less deserved than ever!

He next addressed the gathering: 'The direction chosen by any Government or an individual remains of cardinal importance. No nobility, no self-sacrifice, no energy on the wrong road will finally avail one iota. Idealists should remember this—' and he turned his glance upon me for a second. 'At the end of the day the value of an Emperor or an individual resides in the same factor: have these given their all? None can give more than this. Less will not justify existence. What has been Napoleon's objective—his secret destination throughout?' The Sultan paused, pleasantly he appeared to query space. 'France or Napoleon Bonaparte? We are now in a position to decide that this man no longer represents France but his own mania. Unhappily for Europe and the East, he is still in the saddle there. That he will be thrown is inevitable—as evil also spawns its own end.'

At that Mustapha stepped forward. 'But, Sire, time presses. The French influence has long been detested in this city—'

'Only—by a section of its community,' the Sultan said calmly. 'It has ever been the genius of the Turkish people to absorb, without rancour, such good as can be got from any foreign influence.'

For the first time Mustapha himself showed a trace of excitement. 'Sire, this morning the Janissaries again threatened to set fire to the city.'

'What!' the Sultan exclaimed with a touch of mockery. 'Has the Treaty of Tilsit already been made public?'

'Your Imperial Majesty is pleased to joke,' and Mustapha's smile was wry. 'No, the Janissaries are in a ferment for a rumour has reached them that the Bulgarians are on the march to Stamboul, led by Bairactar of Rustchuk—' he bit out that name.

'We fail to see why Our esteemed ally should wish to pay Us a State visit unannounced.'

There was a second of checkmate, then Mustapha drew himself up, but spoke now with obvious effort: 'Sire . . . it is whispered that Bairactar and his army advance by Imperial Command.'

'Mustapha,' the Sultan said suavely, 'you seem to be better informed than We are. Why should your Sultan need aid from Bairactar?'

This simple question had a disconcerting effect on the Prince. He appeared to be momentarily taken aback: 'Sire . . . Sire, how should this humble servant know?'

'How indeed! This Audience is at an end. Ali Mirza, your services are registered in Our memory.'

The Sultan folded his hands and gazed aloofly into space. The Kisslar Agassi stepped forward, bowed to the three persons of the Persian party who, in turn, made their salutation to the Throne before taking their leave . . ..

As they disappeared Mahmoud said urgently: 'Sire, may I have a word alone with Balthazar?'

Somewhat formally the Sultan replied: 'His Highness will see you in his own chamber,' and as they left by the side entrance, he signed to me to remain beside him. Then he issued a brief word of command and the two Throne courtiers, accompanied by the third courtier before the Veiled Empress's Throne, also withdrew. He and I were alone but for the deaf-mute Nubian slaves in the background—

Barely had the three Throne courtiers marched away than the Sultan stepped impatiently from his Throne and took my hand.

'Sire—you know what jealousy this has caused before . . . was it wise to dismiss the Throne attendants?'

For answer he embraced me. 'Naksh, in the course of years you have become afraid of everyone *but* the Sultan! We are uncertain if this is to Our Advantage!' He led me to the visitors' divan nearby. 'It is a Sultan's whims that keep him sane—not court etiquette.'

Seated beside him, I gazed into his face. 'Their dreadful venom! For months I hope, I try to believe that Mustapha and his mother are reconciled to me and Mahmoud. Then out the poison comes. Yet, heaven knows, this time it is justified! Oh, Sire, that vile Treaty of Tilsit . . . How stoically you sustained the news. France's shame is mine—' and I covered my eyes with my hands.

Briskly he said, 'Today's news was no news to Us,' and he took my hands from my face. 'Earlier Our Greek agents secretly informed Us of the event. We did not wish to sadden you sooner than we had to.'

Reproachfully I looked up: 'You kept this burden from me?'

'There has been a graver anxiety, and a much more immediate one. Tonight it may not be possible to join you. Listen carefully. This news must be broken quickly because of an unforeseen event. But have no fear—the emergency has been met. There has been a plot to assassinate the Sultan and proclaim Mustapha!'

In horror I recoiled, but firmly he held my hands. Gasping for breath I whispered, 'They would not dare—the Sultan's life is sacred.'

'Only while he is alive,' he said dryly. 'We do assure you of that! Mustapha would be safe though he contrived both Mahmoud's death and mine—for the Turks fatally believe that with the last blood of Osman, the Empire will perish. Mustapha as the sole survivor would reign. So he and his mother have reasoned.'

Still stammering with shock I said: 'Have you told Mahmoud?'

He gave a short laugh. 'Mahmoud told me! Come, We shall have no more secrets from you. For a year now Mahmoud, incognito, has secretly visited the city by night. Trained by an adept, he brought this news back. At once couriers were privately dispatched to Bairactar. He and his army, twenty thousand strong, have already crossed the frontier. We hoped for him last night, but in yesterday's heat the going would be hard—' Rising, he faced the arched window beyond. 'At any moment now you will hear their cheerful fifes and drums.'

I rose too, but my voice was still trembling. 'Sire,

who was this adept who trained Mahmoud to visit the city alone, unprotected?'

Turning, the Sultan placed both his hands on my shoulders and spoke half sadly. 'Naksh, your son was safe in these hands. How often the Sultan has himself made that self-same journey into the streets, the cafés, the bazaar! In search of truth. Come, be yourself and smile!' Gently he wheeled me round until we faced the Throne of the Veiled Sultan, his mother. 'One day you will grace that Throne, but by natural events! Absurd Creature, do not tremble. It is inevitable. You are years younger than He who adores you! But be warned, for in absence He will expect more than courage from you. A smiling strength! Remember that, Empress Best Beloved!'

Passionately I exclaimed, 'Never, never call me Empress! It appalls me to think of any life without you.'

He smiled. 'When that time eventually comes, We shall still hope to make Ourself felt! Yes, Empress Best Beloved, that title will yet bring you your greatest happiness. We shall see to it that the name is not whispered, nor yet chanted, but delivered to you as a matter of fact—as befits the message of a realist. One who is ever down to earth! From Arcturus itself—'

As he placed his arm around me, I faced now in the opposite direction of the Thrones . . . suddenly I stiffened, for a second I believed myself to be dreaming. In the background the nearest Nubian slave still stood motionless against his pillar but his head was already fallen forward on his breast. He had been garrotted. I tried to speak but my mouth dried—

The Sultan turned his head slightly and saw what I saw. Quietly he said, 'Remain where you are. Keep calm—all will be well. Do not move—'

He moved, unhurried, to his Throne and at the wall beside the dais he pulled a heavy gold rope. A bell could be heard ringing in the room adjoining our end of the audience chamber. By the time the Sultan had stepped back beside me, Mahmoud had hurried in from the side entrance, followed by the Kisslar Agassi. In a low voice the Sultan said:

'Do not look at the back of the hall. The Nubian guard has been murdered. Each slave is roped to his pillar. Balthazar, leave now with Mahmoud through the Veiled Empress's Throne—hide him in the Seraglio—'

'Sire,' Mahmoud whispered, 'I implore you—come!'

'*Silence* . . . obey.'

Deliberately the Kisslar Agassi held open the curtain of the Veiled Empress's Throne—for an instant his eye flashed at Mahmoud. Mahmoud slowly passed up the steps and the Kisslar Agassi followed him.

The Sultan had turned, smiling as if all this were the most natural thing in the world. Again he took me in his arms as if to embrace me— In my ear he said: 'Every minute that passes quietly now is a minute gained for Mahmoud. Remember that. Balthazar knows what to do next. Any moment now Bairactar will be here, and those devils executed. Beloved, your future is secure—now you too must pass through the Empress's Throne Room—walk calmly through the curtains. We are watched. Balthazar has left the door open at the back of her Throne—follow the passage into the Seraglio.'

'No,' I said, and for the first and last time in my life knew that I was as strong as he was, 'I will not go.' Staring at me now, he knew this too.

Frowning, he whispered: 'Then remain behind the curtains, on her Throne. Neither look, nor listen, nor emerge till We summon you. Unless you obey, you may endanger all our lives. *Vow obedience.*'

Aghast, I whispered: '*I vow.*'

As I turned to the Empress's Throne, suddenly there could be heard distinctly from the Palace gates the military music of Bairactar's army—no muffled Janissary kettledrums but the oboes, fifes, drums and cymbals of victory.

Below his breath I heard the Sultan exclaim: 'Allah be praised! In five, ten minutes now—'

I stepped behind the curtains. In the gloom I

stumbled towards the Throne, I sank upon it as I had promised—I waited . . . At first in this sultry obscurity there was only silence—

And so I did not see that which was later to be known by all. The Sultan walked deliberately to the steps of his throne and then took up a standing position with his right foot on the first step, facing the pillars that led to the back of the Chamber—his hand on the dagger in his sash, his body between the Veiled Empress's Throne and any who might enter.

Barely could he have done so than twelve silent figures entered from the back of the Chamber walking four abreast with swift precision—officers of the Janissary militia. They wore the uniform, the tall, severe head-dress that has no equal. As they approached the Sultan with noiseless, ordered intent—without a word spoken and with a precision matched only by its speed the twelve figures spread to close in a double fan around him. Then, as one, the twelve leaped upon him—

Petrified, I heard this sudden, unspeakable scuffle . . . Powerless to move, I next heard footsteps departing with the same noiseless order with which they must have come. Then silence again . . . .

I rose, I parted the curtains, I went out into the empty Audience Chamber—

The Sultan's body lay in front of his Throne, his life-blood flowing from him. As I flung myself down beside him I believed him to be dead, and my horror had all the fears of a lifetime fulfilled—

At that moment he opened his eyes, he saw me. He raised his right hand slightly . . . Hoarsely, sternly, by a superhuman effort he gave his last command: 'Arcturus!'

# 16. AFTERMATH

THE first to discover us was General Bairactar. He and his men had passed through the Outer Gate without difficulty, although the absence of any guard astonished him. The Middle Gate was partially closed, but an entrance was quickly effected—and to his amazement there too he saw no guard, officer or slave, for all had fled to the underground passages. It was an abandoned habitation. Finally confronted by the Sacred Door, and his consternation mounting, he ordered the brazen panels to be burst open . . . The deserted Seraglio, its silent pavilions, palaccs and gardens lay before him—

He rushed first through one hall, then another . . . In the Audience Chamber he at last found us. Later I heard that this hardened warrior had openly wept when he saw the Sultan—shedding those tears that were to be forever beyond me now . . .

The rest is history—to be later scanned by any schoolchild: of how Prince Mahmoud, flying for his life through the Seraglio, was hidden in a disused chimney in my bath house, where he mounted to the roof unseen with only three minutes to spare before the assassins entered. By next day the story of how these three minutes were gained was known throughout Stamboul—the story of the only slave who had remained on duty—an heroic woman who seized a brazier of blazing coal beside the bath-house furnace and flung it full in the faces of the first Janissaries to enter—an elderly woman henceforth to be known as the Powerful. Blanche was to bear the scars of that blazing brazier on her hands as long as she lived. Yet because Blanche was Blanche, her timing and her strength had been one with her indomitable will, and she herself miraculously escaped death from the assailants as the Janissaries, stumbling over their blinded forerunners, rushed on through the palace in their vain search . . . .

Yet the schoolchild hastily skimming history can never equal the speed or sum of events that crowded through that fearful day when Bairactar of Rustchuk's army imposed order, imprisoned Mustapha and the Persian Kadine, and pacified Stamboul, frantic with grief over the murder of the Sultan, for at five o'clock the cannons were thundering the proclamation of Mahmoud as Padishah . . . .

That evening another audience was held in the Audience Chamber, at which I was instructed to appear, heavily veiled. More dead than alive, it mattered nothing to me where I went, where I was . . . Like a spectre I was led into the Audience Chamber, now filled with Councillors of State and the officials of Bairactar's army.

Before the Throne, on its step, stood Mahmoud with the Grand Cordon of the Osmanli across his breast. He was dressed in the uniform of chief-marshal of the army. Quite clearly, quite coldly I noted all this. The Kisslar Agassi stood at his right hand. It was like some terrible dream, distinct yet disastrous, in which the right people are all in the wrong place. Too late now, General Bairactar stood in the place of honour before the Sultan—

The General was announcing in a voice that all could hear:

'Sire, order has been restored, the Janissaries quelled, the instigators of the murder imprisoned, the assassins dispatched. The city, distraught with grief at the death of their Sultan, fill every street and court. Your Imperial Majesty will now be treasured as Stamboul's own life.'

White-faced, Mahmoud replied: 'Peace has been bought here at the price of its noblest soul. May We live to be more worthy of him—'

As he spoke, there could be heard from the outer courts and grounds of the Seraglio the shouts of the assembled: 'Padishah! Chok Yasha! Mahmoud . . . Mahmoud . . . Padishah! Chok Yasha—'

At that cry of *The Sultan may he live forever*—I was back again on a youthful, sun-struck afternoon years ago with summer still before me . . . My present apathy was pierced with agony—I almost fell.

It was Mahmoud who caught my shoulders, whispering hurriedly: 'My Mother—we are not alone! You must take heart. Tomorrow must be met—'

I forgot the crowded Chamber, the State occasion which meant nothing to me. Hoarsely I said: 'Let me leave—I shall not survive your father's death.'

At this, Mahmoud must have turned to the Kisslar Agassi—for now he held my arm. Softly he said, and in his old form of address: 'Gentle Lady, at first sorrow overwhelms but there is enough love in your past to furnish any future.'

'No,' I whispered, at last aware that the assembly stood silent but observant, 'my life is ended. I beg to retire at once—'

Swiftly, inflexibly Mahmoud whispered back: 'You cannot retire. As Veiled Sultan you have no choice but to proceed—and *at once*. You no longer belong to yourself or—' his voice shook for a second—'another. You belong to the Empire—you must obey.'

'Obey!' my voice rose, 'I cannot.'

'My Mother,' he whispered sternly, 'Our friends gathered around Us await your accord. The kettle-drums of the Janissaries are silenced at last. For this *he* fought, for this he died. Let Us both respond to his bugle *now*—'

He stepped back from me for a second and then held out his hand to me before the assembly—

Slowly I moved forward. As I did so there was a flourish of trumpets. Hand in hand with Mahmoud, I found myself walking to the Throne of the Veiled Sultan, but alone I mounted the steps—

By unseen attendants the inner curtain of the Throne was momentarily opened for me. At the last visible step I turned like an automaton and bowed to Mahmoud, then to the Council—and the curtain fell, concealing me for the rest of my life from both Court and Seraglio . . . .

# 17. THE THRONE OF THE VEILED SULTAN

FOUR strenuous years passed . . . but years that were, inwardly, to me empty as an echo.

Yet the solitary chamber of the Veiled Sultan remained a hive of industry, and as behind its crimson velvet curtains it must surely be one of the most astonishing in the world, I shall describe it for you lest a later date finds it changed beyond recall.

My first clear impression of the Throne-Sanctuary was that it resembled the interior of some vast ruby, its facets glittering with distant light from the gold lattices which surround the Throne itself, revealing the Seraglio court on one side and on the other, the Empress's palace gardens and, across their cypresses, the sea. These lattices were lined with crimson velvet and the Court assembled below the audience-lattice never glimpsed the Empress—only the red velvet steps outside, mounting steeply to the lattice-screen. But the hidden Empress could both see and hear her audience clearly.

Half-way to the lofty Throne, inside the Chamber,

was a narrow Council-table with two seats. One was for the Sultan, but the greater part of the time the Empress spent there alone, transacting her endless business—like a queen bee at the centre of the hive, in the perpetual solitude of majesty, controlling her domain.

In the past, I had never been able to think of the late Empress's life without a shudder—cut off visibly from the Court itself and normal social existence, a living death, as it had seemed to me. But in a short time a curious fact became evident: I had certainly vanished visibly from Court and Councillors, from all but my immediate family—yet into an intimacy with the Seraglio, a sphere of influence unimagined by me before.

The complex of the Seraglio's existence, now that I was aloof from it, was laid before me in detail—with all that was entailed in the administration of its mosques, palaces, pavilions, hammams, pleasure-gardens, stables . . . every institution, indeed, from Council chambers, libraries, hospitals to cook-and-confectionery houses, together with the living quarters of physicians, eunuchs, odalisques and slaves. Not all these came under my jurisdiction but a great many did, and this welter of information was set before me while I was still stunned by grief. The wisdom of this instant burden I can now value to the full.

Mahmoud naturally recovered long before I did,

but even he was never to be the same again. His energetic face was to bear always in repose a self-contained melancholy. Foreign ambassadors were later to record that in his stoic regard there was a sadness that held and haunted the observer. This too was strengthened, I am certain, by the relentless steps he was often compelled to take to ensure reforms. The Janissaries temporarily quelled by Bairactar were to rise again and yet again as years passed—an evil focus for any group of malcontents bent on the disruption of progress. In time Mahmoud was forced to realize that their extermination by himself at the head of his loyal troops might be the only solution. But that day was not yet . . . and meantime there were certain breathing-spaces at home, although our enemies abroad kept the Divan in a ferment of negotiation. Year in, year out, I watched Mahmoud weather every difficulty although at a tremendous cost of energy and anxiety. Yet with all his vigour, he was never precipitate. He planned to replace the turban with the fez years before he ordained this. When first he spoke of it I thought secretly, sadly of the Chief Librarian, the epitome of dignity and grace in his turban, and at once exclaimed: 'This is to banish the tulip from the garden in favour of a brisk array of snapdragon—I'll abdicate!' We could still laugh heartily together, although the creature I had been seemed now as remote as another being. My daughter was an example to me in spiritual calm. Now the Sultana Esmé, she had been tragically widowed five years earlier in the early death of Kutchuk Hussein Pasha, a soldier and statesman of genius. It was, in fact, partly due to him and his troops that Napoleon was defeated at St Jean d'Acre—a crucial failure for Napoleon, as was later plain. Yes, the courage of my children and their devotion to one another sustained me, and I grew to love Adile, Mahmoud's Kadine, as if she were my own daughter—

There were many blessings . . . and yet I was no longer completely with the young people or myself. As I gradually emerged from nightmare I found that the certainty, the assurance of the spirit had gone from me in the horror, the shock of the Sultan's death. I remembered those words of the poet Nizami which the Sultan had once quoted to me, before I understood the burden of his life . . . Now I too felt like a soul in a dead body, *but not journeying with the caravan, or one of its company.*

He had gone—and there was no vestige of contact.

The awareness of the poet Nizami was all I shared with him now—the awareness that I moved through the desert alone . . . .

So things stood for me in my hidden heart four years later—in the early spring of 1812, a year that was to prove of dynamic importance for East and West.

On a certain afternoon I sat, as usual, alone at my

Council-table in the Throne-Sanctuary. I had many plans for the future but at present I was hard at work on routine matters, with no idea then that this particular day would yet prove one of the most momentous in world history—and through the Veiled Throne.

Nowadays, for greater ease at my desk I wore a minimum of drapery—a trim Zouave bolero from which the sleeves and trousers of my dress emerged in soft full petals. But on my head there was always a richly jewelled fez, worn—so Blanche assured me—with true French chic. My curls, in this my forty-ninth year, were now frosty fair, but I had not gained in weight, and my children flattered me by insisting that I looked more like their sister . . . Nor could I ever understand how all that I had felt should leave so little mark on this outer mask. Where was the soul that had once agonized? Was it dead too? And sometimes I would ponder the prophecy of the Martinique seer which had already come true in every detail for Joséphine and for me. She had stated that I would die at the height of my happiness . . . that then my life would pass from this world like a dream. Undeniably I was still here . . . What further happiness could I expect now? And how could it possibly be greater than that which I had already known—and lost?

With a sigh I turned back to the documents before me. Again I summoned resolution for my task as Reverend Mother would have counselled: *do not reject what is in hand to dream of something else . . .*

Suddenly I started—there was a click like the Convent shutter moving back . . . but it was only the Grand Vizier outside the Council lattice . . .

At once I seated myself upon the Throne—for there, above him, I could see him clearly through the Council lattice on my right-hand side—although all he saw through this was the distant sunlit balcony on my left.

'We are ready,' I announced, 'to hear the list of engagements for tomorrow.'

Bowing behind the lattice, he at once read from his parchment:

'Your Imperial Majesty, the State Secretaries will present themselves as usual after your six-o'clock breakfast. Two hours later the Kisslar Agassi arrives with the Harem report. The governors of the new hospital have an audience before noon. Our Sublime Padishah hopes that Your Imperial Majesty will also see a deputation of Bath-house Beauties who are accused of repeatedly tossing one of the eunuchs into the pool. These ladies have twice all but drowned the eunuch in question—so it is said. But Our Sublime Padishah states that the rights and wrongs of this mystery are quite beyond him. At three o'clock European time there is an audience long sought by the French Ambassador. Our Padishah desires your views.'

Calmly I said: 'Cancel the French Ambassador.'

'Imperial Majesty—shall any reason be given to the French Minister?'

For a moment I smiled into space. 'Europe still believes that we are steeped in superstition. Give him a reason he can believe. Inform the French Ambassador that We regret that the Stars are not at present propitious for this pleasing encounter.'

'Does he receive the usual Tokens of consideration?'

'Every courtesy, but no sherbet, no perfume, no scarf.'

'At four o'clock there is an audience long and passionately sought by the English Ambassador.'

'Cancel that also,' I said, 'with a reason *he* can credit. Tell the English Ambassador that the Sultan has gone hunting. Afford him not only courtesy but the Tokens of consideration—sherbet, perfume, scarf. Indicate, although without specific assurance, that the future belongs to all.'

'Imperial Majesty, is it in order to replace these two audiences by the Turkish Scholastic Committee and the Harbour Guild?'

'It is. But put the teachers last or they will argue all day.'

'Alas, there are two further items! The two Hyacinth Bulb Growers of Stamboul are once again in acrimonious dispute as to which shall supply the Seraglio with next year's Heavenly

Blue and Celestial Harmony. Our Sublime Padishah feels that this annual squabble should now be left perennially to the Empress's tender tact.'

'The Empress is flattered. But the only way to deal with these troublesome twins is to separate them. The gardens of the Selamlik do not concern the Empress. She can adjudicate only for those of the Harem. Tenderly, tactfully she returns one squalling infant to the Divan.'

The Grand Vizier gave a slight cough. 'Regrettably the Divan has a further domestic issue today. The city discovers it has been consuming an inferior quality of charcoal at increased cost—as compared with that enjoyed and supplied by the rural community. This has gone on for some time and the city—now inflamed by its own past ignorance—demands excessive fines. The Divan suggests that the Empress impose a lesser fine on the sinners—while conveying that gracious balm to the injured for which she is renowned.'

Unseen by the Grand Vizier, I stuck my quill which I still carried behind my ear and rubbed my hands with mock gusto, while replying staidly:

'By the time We have finished with the sinners *they* will need the balm. That audience will close tomorrow's list, for which We thank you. . . Today's documents are ready—' Lightly I struck a gong beside me and the two slaves, each in his white turban, tunic, and trousers on my side of the lattice dropped the red velvet curtain over the Council lattice—then they advanced to the Council-table, lifted two locked portfolios, saluted me . . . and disappeared with the documents through the door at the back of the Throne-Sanctuary.

From the silent garden on my left came the contented crooning of white fan-tailed pigeons.

Another day begins at sunset, I thought. That is Turkish law. There's no release from time . . . ah, Reverend Mother, behind this lattice I too have learned how *not* to weep—

At that moment, from the garden, Blanche moved on to the balcony—and set sherbet on the balcony table . . . much more slowly than of old. With age she had lost much weight, but she was still hale enough—

'Majesty!' she announced in the same summary way that once she had said Mamzelle, 'sherbet's on the table.'

'Bring it here, please.'

'No, Majesty, that I won't, and that's flat. You come right down off that roost into the sunshine, or what's left of it. Leave these botheration papers—'

Obediently I rose and seated myself at the balcony table, with my back to the Throne-Sanctuary. With another sigh I said: 'These papers help me to forget.' It was the first time I had ever made such an admission, and inwardly only I added: to forget that when the star Arcturus is blotted out, it leaves a greater gap than would the sun.

'Forget?' Blanche exclaimed sharply. 'That the good Lord gave you more than twenty years of joy—with that angel Sultan? And now a sturdy son to keep you busy still?'

I hesitated, but only for a moment—then I leaned across the table and almost beseechingly said: 'Blanche, only to you dare I admit it—for to admit the silence of the past four years seems to confirm it. . . But how I long, oh, how I long for some sign from *him* . . . some glimpse—some ghostly evidence. Anything!'

'No, no, Honey. They don't come back. You've got to go forward.'

'But Blanche, other mourners have had glimpses of the celestial world, or have been comforted. Why should I, with so much love, so many prayers, have no sign? The Kisslar Agassi Balthazar died two years ago and I often feel that he is near. Reverend Mother, who died at Nantes so long ago, I sometimes think is not afar. But from my heart's Beloved there is only absence.'

'Honey, Honey, the answer's as plain as the nose on my face! That sainted Sultan met a martyr's death—and you saw it. You're still bidding him goodbye, 'stead of singing loud and clear: Angel, here I come—on the wings of every morning, like the dawn returning.'

Despite myself, I was arrested by her words. 'If only I could believe this! If only you were right—'

'Of course I'm right, Majesty. In the Lord's good time and sure as death is life, you'll get your sign. When that sad soul of yours is ready for it. Not before. Drink the sherbet while it's cool.'

At that moment, unseen by me, Mahmoud entered by the Throne-Chamber, signed to Blanche for silence, and on a bound covered my eyes with his hands:

'Woman, guess who?'

I laughed. 'That scamp of a son, Mahmoud the Midget!' for this was his family title from the day he had inquired at the age of six: am I really Mahmoud the Great?

'Impossible to surprise her,' he told Blanche. 'Not a tremor, We swear! A woman of iron.'

'No,' I said lightly, 'simply a creature minus her heart—and, so, a stranger to fear.'

With a shake of her head, Blanche left us—

When Mahmoud and I were alone together, or with Blanche, we always spoke in French. Urgently, imperatively now I turned to him:

'Have you had a reply?'

'Yes, it has come. The Czar cannot believe in Our offer of friendship. And why should he—when together with France We hold him in a cleft stick? How *can* he believe in Our friendship when enmity would cost Us less?'

'Just wait,' I said quickly, 'I've thought of a better plan to gain his consent. I will show you. Let's get back to the writing-table—'

But as I rose in haste, my sherbet half finished, Mahmoud caught my hand:

'My Mother, can you not take this project more easily?'

'No!' I said shortly. 'I can never forget that your father's last years were darkened by France's betrayal of Turkey. Was it not for my sake that Napoleon was forgiven again and again? For this I can never forgive myself. Blind fool that I was!'

I sat down at the Council-table and Mahmoud at once seated himself on my right, at the head of it.

Swiftly I said: 'I know you doubt the wisdom of trusting the English. Nor do I believe that England has any genuine feeling for Us, but the fact remains that England *alone* has not succumbed to Napoleon. Nor has England once wavered in her detestation of his rule.'

Elbow on table, his head resting on his hand, Mahmoud reflected. 'That is a fact,' he agreed. 'We may trust England so far.'

'As We may trust Napoleon's vanity,' my laugh was curt. 'He is incapable of sacrifice—so he will never suspect that We can make one . . .' and I opened an old leather case.

'What a shabby portfolio,' Mahmoud interrupted. 'It shall be replaced tomorrow.'

'It can never be replaced,' but I laughed more cordially now. 'It is priceless. It was a gift from my fairy godfather, the Dey of Algiers! He sent me as a slave to Turkey—and may he be forever blessed for that! Inside there is another case, shabbier still—the parting gift of the Convent at Nantes.'

Reverently Mahmoud exclaimed, 'My Mother—these relics shall be treasured.'

'A little less of the relic, please,' I said firmly, 'heirloom has a livelier ring! It contains the next chapter of my story—a project entitled,' and coldly I scrutinized the paper I had drawn out, '*The Downfall of Napoleon Bonaparte.* Shall I read the latest facts?'

'Proceed.'

Aloud I read as follows: 'Five years ago Napoleon was warned by Our cousin, the Empress Joséphine: *I am your wife, I have been crowned by you in the presence of the Pope. I will not voluntarily renounce these honours. If you divorce me all France shall know that it is you who send me away, and shall be ignorant neither of my obedience nor of my profound grief.*'

I paused for a moment, then read on ironically: 'Three years later Napoleon obtained a divorce on the grounds of one omission in their marriage rites, an omission secretly secured by himself. Napoleon then married Marie Louise, Archduchess of Austria, and last year his son was born. In preparation for fresh conquest, further slaughter, Napoleon has now sent this insolent challenge to Russia: *I still hope we shall not spill the blood of thousands of brave men simply because we cannot agree as to the colour of a ribbon!'*

At that point, Mahmoud took a paper from his tunic. 'Today you may add this sensational fact to your record. It reached Us less than an hour ago. It is a copy of the Czar's instructions to Narbonne: "Say clearly to Napoleon that he may cross the Niemen, but never will I sign a peace treaty dictated on Russian territory . . . Even though he were master of Moscow I would not in the least consider my cause lost."'

'Bravo!' and my face lit up, 'nor will Russia's cause be lost.'

Mahmoud shook his head. 'But the rest of the world is mesmerized by this madman! The masses believe he will prevail. Many of Our own people think that Napoleon cannot be beaten. Though they detest it, they desire Our uneasy alliance with France to continue. Fiercely they will resist in Our neutrality in the coming struggle. If it be known that We contemplate an alliance with Russia and England, it will cause insurrection in the city. Perhaps throughout this country. Russia herself cannot credit an offer of friendship. The Czar's ministers are highly suspicious of Our envoys.'

Passionately I exclaimed, 'Then waste no further energy on them—now that time presses, with Napoleon already at Dresden! If this man is to be trapped and ruined, you cannot afford to trust your own Ministers, let alone Russia's! I told you I had a plan. Look at this map!'

As he bent over it, I said: 'I have devised a trap. And at this point—' I tapped the map with my quill, 'Bucharest! The Russian Army of the Danube is superior to any other they possess. Its Generals are the hard core of Russia's military power. At Bucharest, General Kutusoff is stationed, with officers as seasoned as himself. There We shall dispatch a special Envoy with Our secret Treaty.'

Mahmoud was aghast. 'But this is not according to protocol! And why should the Generals credit what their Ministers cannot?'

'Because the Generals know how many beans make five on their own field! And Kutusoff knows us both. Also We shall offer certain sacrifices that later in the hour of victory this country will be readier to make. The Czar will listen to his Generals *—he will have to!*'

Mahmoud rose—he stood staring across to the distant sunlit balcony and spoke with the exasperation that betrays tension, excitement. 'The plan is too simple, much too simple!'

'That's its strength,' I retorted. 'It carries its own solution. The Czar *must* listen to his Generals!'

Abruptly Mahmoud turned to me. 'By heavens, you are right. The plan has genius. And if it works—'

'I have only one anxiety,' I said calmly, 'the

imperative need for secrecy until Napoleon is bogged in Russia and the trap sprung.'

But Mahmoud was again staring into space. 'Yes . . . yes, with the release of the Army of the Danube from Our frontiers, the deed could be done!' Again he turned abruptly to me: 'My Mother, for the first time in my life you have terrified me! If We can convince General Kutusoff—' he sat down eagerly.

'Of course We can convince Kutusoff! He is a soldier, a man of action as well as of vision. He will not waste an hour, for he knows us both. He will be enchanted!'

'It is settled,' Mahmoud said briefly. 'Our Envoy will leave tonight—' Suddenly his gravity was released in a robust laugh. 'What, oh what will the Czar finally make of it?'

'What will the Czar make of it?' Gaily I stuck my quill behind my ear and folded my hands in State-pomp: 'The Czar will make Kutusoff a Prince, of course!' Then I grew serious again. 'For on that day the East and Europe will be rid of a man who is a malady, a disease that has overtaken the world.'

I looked up, thinking how like his father Mahmoud looked, yet how unlike . . . and I smiled with a touch of lost coquetry. 'On that memorable occasion,' I announced, 'The Sultan will also reward the Veiled Empress . . . Yes, on *her* he will bestow—a kiss!'

# 18. THE SULTAN'S PACKMAN

DESPITE our haste, our every precaution, and my conviction that General Kutusoff would not waste an hour, for weeks on end there were maddening delays, doubts, procrastinations on the part of those we wished to aid until—in a fever of anxiety and later a passion of despair—we feared that the treaty we proposed with Russia would never be signed at Bucharest. Our difficulties were doubled by the complete secrecy in which Mahmoud and I worked. Not one of our Ministers suspected what was afoot. Indeed, our Foreign Minister was now in receipt of repeated proposals from France by which Turkey could secure the return of all former territory 'not in exchange for any alliance to continue the war against Russia, but merely on the Sultan's word that if and when Turkey made peace with Russia, France should be promptly informed'. It required every ingenuity to persuade our Foreign Minister that this tempting offer could not be dealt with at present . . . that silence was the Sublime Porte's only reply. The ignorance of the other Embassies in Stamboul was complete, for their Ministers and attachés remained wholly dependent on their interpreters—and these were all Stamboul dragomen! It was a fantastic situation for the Padishah, with his inborn reverence for protocol, and chafed him sorely, but once his resolve had been made, he never wavered. Our two secret Envoys, the most reliable we had, were worn out by ceaseless journeying in and out of Bulgaria. When hope died abruptly, first with Mahmoud, then with me, grimly we still urged the matter on, from some blind determination stronger than ourselves . . . until the incredible did take place and on May 17th the preliminary treaty was signed at Bucharest . . . On May 28th the Treaty of Bucharest was secretly signed there in its final form. Only then, with the return of our Envoy, did we realize how completely General Kutusoff had been with us—how much he had had to surmount . . . .

Later, an impressive fact was noted by informed persons about this date, the 28th of May. It was the final day of Napoleon's period at Dresden, the apogee of his career, when he received the assembled homage of the Sovereigns of Austria, Prussia, Bavaria, Saxony and Westphalia. Before sunrise next day he was on the march with an army of six hundred thousand men to subdue the widest empire in the world. The Niemen was crossed at the end of June and Vilna occupied. In clouds of stifling summer dust, through deserted steppes and forests the Grande Armée advanced . . . with the Russians under Barclay de Tolly retreating without battle until mid-August, when both armies engaged outside Smolensk. This victory was celebrated by the French in the destruction of Smolensk; and it was at this point that Napoleon made his momentous decision to push on to Moscow for his winter headquarters. But Borodino lay between him and the Holy Russian City. Borodino with General Kutusoff in command—and the final loss of seventeen thousand Frenchmen dead or wounded and forty-three French Generals slain or disabled. Another costly victory, as the Russians, after an infernal struggle, were seen retreating in good order . . . .

Yet the road to Moscow, Napoleon's prize, now lay open. And as the conqueror rode in with his cavalry, a stupefying situation awaited him and one never before witnessed— A deserted city greeted him, peopled only by some hundreds of demented criminals, released before the Russians left . . . .

Within hours of Napoleon's entry, sporadic fires, believed to have been lighted by the convicts, were blazing . . . the wind rose fiercely and in three days half the city was in ruins. But the loot to every man's hand beggared description, as did the quantities of wine, vodka and confectionery! It took a day or so to discover that solid food was alarmingly scarce . . . .

As I write this memoir one year after these events,

and others I shall now describe, there is today a wounded French soldier named Dubosc living comfortably in Stamboul who might have been left to rot in Russia like half a million others had it not been for the connivance of a certain packman, one of Napoleon's oriental couriers—who was also, as could happen, secret agent to the Sublime Porte! The Moscow débâcle has long since become world news, but by reason of these two men's presence in Napoleon's suite, after the fire forced him to vacate the Kremlin, both the Sultan and I were later given a verbatim report of what occurred in the Emperor's presence there . . ..

You may picture, as we did, this particular room in that ruined mansion—its window revealing the September night sky lit by the glare of flames. Periodically, puffs of smoke swept past its tightly shut panes. The room displayed dilapidated grandeur—velvet curtains sagging, an oil painting in a massive gold frame hanging askew, a handsome chair in a corner piled with army greatcoats. Only the wide table in the centre was orderly, with a storm-lamp lighting its papers. Behind it, his back to the window, sat Napoleon Bonaparte, with his secretary on his right, at a smaller table. In this way Napoleon faced the doorway, from which the door had been removed, its heavy brocade portière alone remaining. There was a soldier stationed always at this doorway—tonight, Dubosc was on duty. Except for the storm-lamp on the table, the room was poorly lit and gave the effect of a bivouac. Dubosc, whose first occasion it was there, noted the Emperor with especial interest. He sat, at that preliminary glance, with his head sunk between raised shoulders, a quill idle in his hand, one leg thrust out, the heel of its riding boot dug into the carpet, like that of a man in the throes of a perpetual cramp—

An Aide-de-Camp stood in the centre of the room facing the Emperor, awaiting orders, and the first words that Dubosc heard were these:

'As soon as any courier arrives from Constantinople, show him in. No matter the hour—day or night. This delay has become incredible.'

'Sire!' the Aide saluted sharply. Dubosc saw him disappear into the corridor which was better lit, as there the men off-duty diced or played cards beside the stoves.

Napoleon, his voice rasping with annoyance, had turned to his secretary: 'Write as follows to the Foreign Secretary: You were instructed in July to prevent any possibility of peace between Russia and the Ottoman Empire. You were also instructed that the Turks must at once menace the Crimea with their fleet. The total absence here of any news is disquieting. In that earlier dispatch you were ordered to send special couriers, with utmost speed, every week to Constantinople. Polish officers were cited, our Embassy to demand the guarantee of

Turkey. You would realize the importance of this step. I had it always in my mind to give these orders. I do not know why I did not do so sooner—' he broke off. 'Erase that! No,' he added angrily, 'let it stand! But that I never doubted that the Sultan would in his own interests at once take the field at the head of his troops.' As he spoke, Napoleon rose impatiently, shook himself, and added irritably, 'Any rational being would.'

Nervously his secretary said: 'Do I set down these last words too?'

'No. I am thinking aloud—and before fools this is folly! Yet answer this: what sovereign of Turkey who wishes to remain on his throne dare refuse my offer? As for the Russians—what can their Generals do compared with mine? Pah! They are still in the Bronze Age. Savages who burn their own cities. I have studied the lives of all of them!'

'Indeed, yes, Sire! And probably all has gone as you wish with the Porte—despite this curious silence from Stamboul.'

At that instant there was a sharp rat-a-tat on the jamb of the doorway.

Impatiently Napoleon exclaimed: 'Enter!'

The Aide pushed past Dubosc: 'Sire, an officer from the Salvage Corps has arrived with some papers of importance—discovered in the City's Record Office.'

'Show him in.'

An officer grimed with smoke and dirt entered, saluting smartly. He looked boyishly pleased to bear treasure-trove.

'Well, what is it?' the Emperor demanded.

'Sire, we were just in time—the place was in flames. The very cabinet was smouldering . . . but this document seems intact—except for some soot.' He handed over a large document with a seal dangling from it.

Napoleon took the document, broke the seal, unfolded the pages, and by the light of the storm-lamp scanned its first lines—then, feverishly, its last ones . . .

In a voice shrill with hysteria, 'Hell and damnation!' he exclaimed. Collapsing in his chair, he yelled at the officer: 'Get out!'

The officer hurriedly obeyed but the secretary rose in alarm: 'Sire, what has happened?'

'Read it, read it—no, leave it alone! That infamous paper, stinking of brimstone, is the Treaty of Bucharest!'

Trembling, the secretary could only repeat, 'Bucharest, Sire?'

'Yes, dolt! The treaty between Turkey and Russia. The Sultan and the Czar have struck hands. The incredible has taken place—' He rose in wild disorder, and in his fury brushed a pile of correspondence off the table. 'What man or devil conceived this fiendish alliance?'

As he spoke there was another rat-a-tat and the Aide with beaming face announced:

'Sire, at last! The Courier from Constantinople!'

Haggardly Napoleon stared at a man dressed as a packman, who entered as the Aide left.

The Courier, who appeared to be in the last stages of exhaustion, bowed curtly.

Angrily Napoleon exclaimed: 'You are weeks late.'

'Sire, it is a miracle that I am here at all!' The Courier's tone was cold, his French cultured, and his personality at once sobered the other man. 'Much of my journey has been made on foot. In Stamboul the situation was unchanged at the end of July. The Embassies, still bewildered, vie for the Sultan's ear. The Divan itself is irritable and at a loss, for obdurately the Sultan maintains silence and seclusion. I am, however, able to inform you that Prince Kutusoff, now Supreme Commander of the Russian Forces, is thirty-five miles south of Moscow. Not only can his men already *see* the conflagration, but the gale is actually blowing the ashes over them!' He paused for a moment. Napoleon, still standing, leaned on the table supported by his clenched fist, as if paralysed. Then the Courier added:

'I am also able to report that five hundred miles farther west, the Armies of the Danube are marching north!'

'Anything else?' the query was toneless.

'There is nothing more,' the Courier replied.

Heavily, Napoleon slumped into his chair. Silently his secretary watched him— A second later, nervelessly, Napoleon flapped his hand at the Courier—

The Courier, raising the portière as he left, saw Dubosc at attention, immobile. Dubosc winked . . .

Behind the curtain they could hear the Emperor, in the same hollow voice demanding, with the senseless repetition of a patient in delirium: 'What devil conceived this *coup*? Just tell me that . . . just tell me that—'

Soothingly, his secretary began: 'Sire, the East is proverbial for its cunning. Doubtless the Sultan—'

'That indolent Oriental? Are you an imbecile?' His rage was mounting again. 'There is a *mind* behind this *coup*. It has impudence, strength, genius. But whose mind? Whose, whose?'

Again his secretary rose in alarm, and again as hurriedly re-seated himself. 'Sire, *as you press the point*—could there be, might there be some woman behind it in Poland or—or Paris? Somebody of importance in the background—possibly with a grudge?'

Violently Napoleon retorted: 'Rubbish, the Empress Joséphine had no more resentment than a pigeon! Women will swallow any pill, no matter how bitter—if it is handsomely gilded. Women are slaves, not strategists. I know every General on the field today. There is only *one* mind that could have conceived such a *coup*—and that is my own. Mine, do you hear?'

Suddenly he rose, smiting the table, and still staring blindly: 'Then who is behind this outrage? Who, who?'

He shouted the last word twice, then in a dead-flat tone, ominous in its quiet, he uttered it the third time: 'Who?'

# 19. MESSAGE FROM ARCTURUS

As the Grande Armée marched month by month nearer Moscow, Mahmoud and I marked time painfully and in a very different exhaustion. That summer and autumn were to prove the most difficult and dangerous period, politically, that we had yet known. The Divan had also become increasingly suspicious and resentful. In July the Russian Ambassador arrived in Stamboul, to the uneasiness of the French and other Embassies who had no idea that a certain Russian Admiral had been in Stamboul for some time. Rumours of the treaty were now in circulation, but at first no Foreign Minister could credit that the Sultan had ratified this—our own Minister least of all. Yet as time went on, the conviction grew in the city . . . and by October, when the news leaked out that Bessarabia had been relinquished in exchange for Russia's confidence, fear and anger mounted with this threat to our vital food supplies from the Danube—as the Russian defeat by Napoleon was still a foregone conclusion in Stamboul. Violent disorders became a daily occurrence.

The Janissaries, vowing the dethronement of the Sultan, revolted and set fire to the city—

At this critical hour, and before the insurrection was fully under way, the first official news of Napoleon's defeat and rout reached the Sublime Porte through the British Embassy. Russia had accomplished that which Europe in concert had failed to achieve . . . Russia and the Ottoman Empire hand in glove. The Treaty of Bucharest was vindicated.

Yet in Stamboul, revolution had been a perilously near thing—and at this stage certain malcontents who persisted in vilifying the treaty were summarily executed . . . a severity in the Sultan that astonished, alarmed and silenced other reactionaries.

The vindication of the treaty was followed by its world-acclamation one month after. On a certain December day, in late afternoon, the Audience Chamber presented a scene of the greatest splendour, and the adjoining reception chambers the unique beauty of their treasures from the old world and the new. Today was one of those ceremonial occasions when, beneath their ten cupolas, some fifteen thousand meals would be prepared in the Seraglio kitchens . . .

In the Audience Chamber, snow whirled across the arched windows; braziers glowed vividly, and the assembled Court was warmly attired in mantles of ermine and sable. Today a rich diversity had further enhanced the pageant, for with the Bulgarians there were now Austrian and Hungarian dignitaries in brilliant national dress. The Divan, as well as the Grand Vizier, stood at the Sultan's right hand, for this was not simply a Court but a State function. The crimson curtains of the Veiled Empress's Throne were already open, and although none could see the Veiled Sultan on her throne, I could see and hear all clearly. Hidden I might be, but this afternoon I was as resplendently attired as the Padishah himself. Indeed, Blanche had assured me only ten minutes ago that today—invisible and all—I certainly looked like someone! And Blanche was not always so indulgent....

The Interpreter was in his usual prominent position—with a little pang I noted that he was no longer the dear old enemy of my arrival twenty-eight years ago, for he had died last spring, but another gifted Greek—and this would be an exacting occasion for him.

As soon as the fanfare for the Padishah ceased, the Grand Vizier declared: 'Your Imperial Majesty, I beg to announce the arrival of His Excellency the British Ambassador!'

'Let him proceed.'

In sonorous tones the Grand Vizier repeated: 'His Excellency, the British Ambassador!'

I heard a brief fanfare and then saw the Ambassador make his dramatic entrance. He did this to the music of the galliard on which the British National Anthem was founded in 1623. As the Ambassador advanced, he made the customary three bows—one, on entering the Presence, one half-way through the Chamber, and the last when he stopped a few feet in front of the throne.

Graciously Mahmoud said: 'The Empress who is present joins Us in this welcome, Excellency! We are delighted to greet you.'

At this the Ambassador took one step to the right and made a profound bow to my lattice.

Mahmoud continued: 'Your cheering dispatch from Russia last month prevented reactionaries firing this city. Now We understand that you have further good news.'

'Sire, I have the best news of all! Fresh dispatches have reached me this morning from Sir Robert Wilson in Russia. I am empowered to inform Your Imperial Majesty that the French débâcle is complete. The Grande Armée has ceased to exist. On the sixteenth of November, the Russians captured Minsk with its huge store of munitions and supplies—Napoleon's last hope in retreat for his starving men. On the twentieth of November, the Russians captured the vital bridge over the Beresina—' He paused for a moment. 'At Beresina the Ottoman trap was sprung! The French found the Army of the Danube waiting for them—with Prince Kutusoff also advancing from their rear.'

Quietly Mahmoud said: 'This news is music in Our ears—' and the Interpreter swiftly repeated the gist in several languages.

Then the British Ambassador made a further announcement: 'Sire, my dispatches state that the Russians won because they could not lose—given that tactical position and the number and ability of those seasoned troops there.'

Mahmoud, I felt, must be inwardly smiling—when suddenly he said:

'Excellency. We would value the Empress's view on this matter!'

I was startled, and my unexpected voice sounded to myself somewhat ghostly, but I hope sweet enough, as I serenely said:

'Something We imagine was also due to silence! In Martinique, We believe they have a proverb: In war do not warn your enemy!'

As the Interpreter tossed my reply to and fro for the benefit of that international assembly there were smiles and some involuntary laughter from our foreign friends.

Then to my astonishment Mahmoud made his pronouncement: 'The Treaty of Bucharest preceded Moscow—preceded the Army of the Danube, preceded Beresina! But a woman's wit preceded all! In the name of that Treaty We salute her now—in a name never to be forgotten: *Bucharest!*'

Fleetly but meticulously the Interpreter translated—and on his final word the assembly responded as one voice, resonant, imperative:

'Bucharest! Bucharest!'

Again Mahmoud addressed the Ambassador:

'And what of Napoleon himself?'

Wryly the Ambassador smiled: 'As a rat leaves a sinking ship, he has fled westward by sleigh. If he is bound for Paris, God help him there!'

Pleasantly, politely Mahmoud replied: 'Allah help him indeed! Continue.'

'He must inform France that the Grande Armée, the mightiest army the world has ever seen, is now a straggling remnant, lost in the blizzards of Poland. He had lost more than three hundred and fifty thousand men in Russia alone, as well as tens of thousands of non-combatants, all his artillery, all his supplies. And he must face the world with a total of human suffering at which the mind reels.'

With calm but deadly precision Mahmoud replied: 'He is anathema. His end is only a matter of time now.'

Again the Ambassador bowed: 'Sire, the British defeat of the Danish Fleet was earlier responsible for the miscarriage of Napoleon's infamous Treaty of Tilsit. Lest there should be any doubt as to Britain's future intentions, I am instructed by His Britannic Majesty's Government to assure Your Imperial Majesty that this is our policy: Respect for the faith of treaties; respect for the independence of nations; respect for the line of policy known as the balance of power; and,last but not least,respect for the honour and interests of our own country.'

'Convey Our satisfaction to His Britannic Majesty,' Mahmoud replied. 'The East has slammed the gate on Napoleon Bonaparte. Europe will bar and bolt it. And now—' he addressed the Grand Vizier:

'Today and tomorrow, in every Mosque let prayers of thanksgiving be offered. Then, and then only, let festivity abound for one day and one night!' Again Mahmoud turned to the Ambassador: 'Excellency, We shall look for you as guest of honour on that glad occasion.'

The Ambassador made his final bow with that austere dignity which is part tradition, part a personal integrity, and he was played out by our regimental band striking up the March from Scipio which, since Handel's day, has been the parade march of the Grenadier Guards . . ..

A few minutes later, he was followed through the pillars by the rest of the Court and I heard Mahmoud instructing the Grand Vizier:

'We wish to speak with the Empress alone. Notify Us when the Thanksgiving procession is ready to start for the Mosque. . . .'

All happiness, I at once dismissed my own Throne attendants and stepped down to my Council-table and our two empty seats which had silently supported so much anxiety, and for so many weary months . . . .

I had not long to wait and there Mahmoud was! Beyond words, we gazed at one another . . . As he kissed my hand I could only repeat: 'His defeat has given peace to the world. At last the nations can rest.'

Dryly Mahmoud retorted: 'Before that siesta takes place he will have to account to France for the wildest extravagance ever known to man. *And* the French are a frugal people, as *We* know!' Laughing, he seated himself beside me, and with our hands still clasped on the narrow table again we gazed long and thankfully at each other. 'Tilsit is avenged,' he said quietly, 'Joséphine is avenged. And you have done it.'

'We were simply instruments . . . and without you, I should have been powerless.'

'My Mother—the plan was yours from start to finish—I only saw it through.'

I laid my hand on his shoulder: 'Mahmoud, more than Tilsit lay behind it for me, and far more than Joséphine. It was a debt I owed your Father—a debt from France—' I laid my other hand on my breast, '*here*, at the heart of the Ottoman Empire.'

Tenderly he smiled. 'That heart so dear to *him* and me! This is the time to tell you that today your official name has been chosen—the one by which you will be known to posterity when this son of yours is only a memory! Today the Divan has been informed that from henceforth you will be known as Empress Best Beloved.'

I stared at Mahmoud . . . in a whisper I said, '*Empress Best Beloved*, but that was his secret name for me! Known only to us both . . . his gift to me before the Throne was mine. What made you choose those words, of all words?'

'They came to me today, in thinking of my Father.'

In wonderment I replied: 'He once said: the title Empress Best Beloved will yet bring you your greatest happiness—' and I repeated the message slowly, like a child remembering a lesson— 'He added, We shall see to it that the name is not whispered, nor yet chanted, but delivered as a matter of fact—as befits the message of a realist who is ever down to earth!'

Joyfully, I raised my face to the dim shadows of the Veiled Throne. 'And today the message reaches me—it is a miracle!'

'It is better than a miracle,' and again Mahmoud laughed, 'it is the restoration of original order—and in the most practical way, for in sending an urgent message does one not choose the swiftest, nearest agent possible, and am I not your son and his?'

As he spoke, the sound of military music reached us from the lattice above the Seraglio court and just then we saw the Grand Vizier approach the Audience lattice.

'Sire, the Thanksgiving procession is ready to start for the Mosque.'

Briefly Mahmoud replied: 'Allah be praised!' and with his customary alertness, left me—

But I was no longer alone and bliss flowed from me in blessing. Arcturus, shrine of meeting, shone today as it had yesterday and would tomorrow. Sightless, yet secure—at last I *knew* . . . .

Down to earth with him now, as befitted a realist, I was suddenly aware of a slight sound at the Audience lattice. The Grand Vizier gave a polite little cough—he had waited behind for a moment to bid me good night. Kindly, courteously he announced:

'Your Imperial Majesty, there is a vast and happy multitude gathered in Stamboul tonight . . . A new era has begun. The snow has ceased and the night is already star-lit. . . .'

*And here the Memoir ends.*